*Kati + Kevin – Nice meeting y'all*
*Goth – sharing – Hope you enjoy*
*the read. Jim Bishop Jr.*

# ORTON

## A NOVEL

## JIM BISHOP JR.

D1571948

**BACK BURNER BOOKS**
MADISON, WISCONSIN

Back Burner Books
Madison, WI 53704
www.BackBurnerBooks.com
info@backburnerbooks.net

Cover design by Hannah Linder Designs
www.hannahlinderdesigns.com

Library of Congress Control Number: 2023905911
ISBN: 978-1-7363341-4-0
First Edition: May 2023

Although two people in this book had existed, in its entirety this book is a work of creative nonfiction. All errors, omissions, and temporal or factual discrepancies are the sole responsibility of the author.

For purchase, or for more information, suggestions or corrections, please contact info@backburnerbooks.net

# Chapters

# Preface

This book arose from a promise made to Peggy Orton. It is entirely fictional and written for a man, my friend, a gentle guy named Jim Orton, Peggy's husband. I worked with Peggy who was the governor's northern representative for Wisconsin. My job as a journalist for another state agency allowed Peggy and I to meet at various state functions. During one of those first gatherings, I sat with her and her husband Jim at a dinner reception. He and I became fast friends. Although 20 years my senior, I learned he was a retired mailman, like my father had been, and that we also shared similar outdoor passions. Over some PBR we shared duck hunting stories, fishing adventures, and life on a rural mail route. Joining them one evening for dinner at their home in Hayward, I was led by Jim into his "reading" room, which was wall to wall books, all westerns, maybe every one ever written. A year or so later Jim came down with lung cancer. Feeling helpless to do something, anything, I wrote Jim into his own western, thus began the first chapter of this novel. Peggy let Jim read it when he came out of surgery. She related to me what a happy effect it had on him. "Jim," she said to me, "you have to promise you will finish that book someday." This is the first novel I've written, and the promise has been fulfilled. It is dedicated to the real Jim Orton, who I also believed, guided my hand in its writing.

# 1

# DILEMMA

A NORTH WIND SWEPT THE QUIET WINTER STREETS OF Hayward, a small town in northwest Wisconsin. In the evening darkness it blew down on a lonely figure stepping from a rusting green pickup. Jack Wayland was chilled. He needed liquid fire to warm his insides. The bottle in the truck had been empty for hours. Across the street the lights of the Moccasin bar caught his eye. Damned February he thought, wishing he was back in the warmth of Arizona. He walked a little faster. He was a long way from home, looking for a man that he hoped would give him answers. A man two cowboys in Malta Montana gifted Wayland with a hint of where the man might be. Railroads led to Hayward.

When Wayland got his answers from this man, he would kill him. He was anxious to find him and deal with him.

An unfamiliar tune echoed off the jukebox. He hated rock and roll. The tables and chairs of the faintly lit saloon were empty. Just like the Stockman's in Yuma, Wayland thought. The last time he was there was five weeks ago ushering in New Year's 1960. Later that night he robbed a drunk whose car had gone into a dry ditch. Drunken dumb bastard, he thought, the guy probably never new I took his money. Wayland laughed at the thought.

He found a place at the bar. The young bartender warily approached her only customer. The worn sun-beaten face under the tan cowboy hat storied this guy from another place in time. She had seen many a fisherman, hunter, and occasional farmer come through here, but this fellow was different.

"I need a shot of Daniels and a beer," Wayland quietly called out.

The bartender stood waiting. She knew there was something else. She'd caught the question in his eyes. Wayland knew too.

"Anything else?" she asked.

"I'm looking for a man named Orton Wayland," he said fingering a scar under his chin. He thought of the whiskey.

"The only Orton I know is Jim, a mailman in town here," she said turning for the bottles.

Wayland stepped away from the bar. He waited in

silence for his drinks at a table near the far wall beneath mounts of big fish. So, Orton had changed his name, taken up a route, that makes sense, getting lost in a town like this. He eyed the big fish mounts. What the hell are they?

The bartender brought the drinks.

"You a friend of Jim's?" she asked.

"Sorta," he replied, "Do you know him?"

"Only that he likes to deer hunt, a quiet guy but damn good with a rifle and..."

Before she could finish Wayland quickly swallowed the Daniels, flushed a few dollars on the table and headed for the door. A rising fear followed. Orton had been good with his hands and a knife and now he knew how to use a rifle. That changed things and he knew he had to act fast.

What Wayland didn't know was that Orton was looking for him – and always had been.

Orton watched Wayland. Inside the newspaper office doorway, he studied this man as he made his way to the green pickup. Old feelings of hatred and dread began to find a way into his heart again, a heart that had only known love for this new country and a family he cherished and would protect with his life. Orton tried to fight a desire to step into the light and call this man out and destroy him. Given the chance, Wayland would have done it to him by now.

A man does not come 2,000 miles to have a drink in a fisherman's saloon. Wayland was there to kill Orton.

Orton knew that. That dusty cowboy would leave only when he's settled that score.

While Orton had lost his fear of dying years ago, he never got over the dying of fear, thinking of the day his brother Jack would return. Even Peggy allowed shadows of this dark secret that haunted Orton's dreams. Because of her love for this man, she gave him time to bury his past. She lived with it and without it.

Lovely, beautiful Peggy. Her hair was graying now but the dark eyes, small girlish figure, and straight cut features of her face were still there. In the cold wind of this Hayward street, Orton saw the warmth of all the past years he had had with her. It shook the hatred from his heart. But he would have to face Wayland or know no peace.

Should death find him, Peggy would never know why. He'd worked so hard at loving her that she had little time to question his past which remained locked inside Orton. Together they lived with this hidden past. It now sat alone in a parking lot as a dry snow began to fall.

Had I my rifle, Orton thought, this could all be over. The rifle was only a few feet away in his own truck. No one would ever know why this cowboy with Montana plates on his pickup was killed in northern Wisconsin. It would be one of those unsolved mysteries. The rifle would never be found much like the knife that lay in the deep sands of the Missouri river in Montana. He full well knew too he could not kill again. Mixed with the silt and sand on that knife was the blood of Carl Wayland, their father.

# 2

# CARL WAYLAND

CARL WAYLAND, THE MAN WHO WOULD EVENTUALLY BE killed by his son, began life in a remote sod hut outside of Bluff City Kansas in 1900. Carl's father was a poorly paid land agent for the government.

When Carl was five years old the family moved to the Fort Belknap Indian Reservation in the middle of Montana. His father took the job as the agent there helping the Gros Ventre Indian tribe in managing land disputes.

Carl went to the native American school where he was often picked on for his small size and white skin. The harassment ended, however, when Joe Littlestar became his friend. Big Joe, a black native American, protected Carl and the two became inseparable. After school they could be found riding tribal horses on the vast lands of the open prairie.

As his father spent long days at the agency and his mother worked in the local dry goods store, there was plenty of time for Joe. Jonathon Littlestar, Joe's father, made a living shooting deer, elk and antelope and selling it to the white markets. He often took Carl and Joe with him on his trips, including camping trips into the Missouri Breaks. Joe's mother went along to skin, butcher and prepare the meat for shipment to the white men.

When Carl was twelve years old and with the Littlestars on a weeklong trip into the Breaks, a number of desperate hungry men came off the plains and paid a visit to Wayland's home. After they left, they had taken food, some money, and made young Wayland an orphan. The men were later captured in Colorado, sent back to Montana, and hung.

With no place to go, Carl was taken in by the Littlestars as one of the family until the day he was handed over to a white family from Livingston. This family, the Heaths, had a large land holding and was trying to make it rich in corn and beans. They needed all the help they could find. Unfortunately, the alkali soils yielded but a few bushels of produce despite the long hours of tilling, watering, and removing the rocks from the fields. Mick Heath, who had come over to America from Ireland, was a determined man and would not give up.

For two years Carl labored under the watchful eye of Heath all the while dreaming of the free and easy life he had once led. At the Heaths homestead there was no time for hunting trips or camping.

One evening after a long day of tilling with a steel hoe, Wayland mentioned to Heath that he wanted to go back to Fort Belknap. Heath could not afford to lose his free labor and beat Wayland almost unconscious. He warned the boy that another beating was forthcoming should he ever mention his leaving again.

That night the youth planned his get-away. A few hours after the house went quiet, he tried to sneak out of his room. He found the door locked from the outside. With a surging rage he was ready to try and break the door down; it took a willful effort to calm himself and work a new plan.

He went along with work the next two weeks as if nothing had happened. He worked hard. He also noticed where Heath left his 30-30 rifle and shells. He also found a screwdriver and while alone in the house managed to loosen the screws of the dead bolt to his room. By pushing a hard wire through to the screws, he knew he could knock the screws out. Another piece of hidden wire behind the bolt would keep it from falling to the floor.

On a night when the winds of Montana blew loud

across the prairie, Wayland made his escape, grabbing the rifle and shells on the way out. A fair trade, he thought, for all the damn work he put into this worthless farm. He traveled north, living off the land, crossing the Missouri at Hay's Ferry and made his way to the familiar Breaks.

A few days after Wayland's escape, Mick Heath pounded his knotty fist on Jonathon Littlestar's door. Littlestar had just returned from a trip downtown when he confronted the angry white man on his front porch.

"Where is he, where is Carl?" Heath asked, "I want him back, and I want him back now!"

Littlestar took a long pull on his recently rolled cigarette and exhaled with a slow smile. He quietly explained to the mad Irishman that Wayland had not come back to Fort Belknap. In his own mind Littlestar suspected Carl was at the Missouri Breaks camp but he would never relate that information to Heath. Littlestar found it a bit amusing and grinned.

"What's so damn funny Indian?" Heath yelled. He tried to strain his neck around to look into the room behind Littlestar. "I'm going to get the sheriff and come back and search every inch of this property and when we find the boy, I'll have you thrown in jail. It won't be so funny then, will it, chief?"

Littlestar had dealt with angry white men. They could be dangerous. It was best to appeal to their needs and

ORTON

Littlestar knew Heath could look forever and not find Wayland on his property.

"Mr. Heath," Littlestar said, "I told you Carl is not here and if you want to search my house and garage right now, please go right ahead." He opened the door and held if for Heath to enter.

Heath took one step in and then quickly stepped back onto the porch. He hesitated, looked into the open doorway and then at Littlestar.

"Okay Indian," he said, "I believe you. The boy's not here but I think you know where he is and I'll be watching you."

"If the boy comes back here," Littlestar said looking directly into Heath's face, "I'll get word to you."

It was the direct straight away look into the big Native American's face that convinced Heath that Littlestar was telling the truth.

"Okay, okay," Heath said, "Good.... okay. I'll leave you and your family alone then. If the boy comes back telegraph me in Livingston. They will get the word to me."

Heath stepped off the porch and walked over to his truck. He opened the door and took a long look at Littlestar standing at the door on the porch. He looked past the house to the weather beaten unpainted garage and found the two indistinguishable. He shook his head, got into the driver's seat, started the engine and drove off in a cloud of red dust.

Littlestar watched him go and when he could not see the truck anymore, he went into the house. Standing to the inside of the door was Bella.

"I'm glad you don't lie to me like that," she said, "I almost believed you myself."

Littlestar looked at her. "It wasn't so much of a lie," he said. "Carl won't be coming back here. Where is Joe?"

Bella started to laugh and said, "He is down at Josie Creek fishing." She stopped and began to grin.

Littlestar's face turn into a broken puzzle of wrinkles. "What?" he asked.

"Joe's fishing with Carl," she said, "I meant to tell you but then that man showed up and...."

Before she could continue Littlestar started to laugh. So did Bella. They both laughed hard and long. When they stopped Littlestar grinned at Bella and said, "You run down to the creek and tell the boys to stay put. I'll start packing for the Breaks and Joe and I'll will be gone for a couple of days, and we'll have to pack enough food for Carl for a long stay. We'll leave tonight after dark. If anyone asks where Joe and I are, tell them I'm on one of my hunting trips."

Littlestar did a check down the roadway and told Bella to go. After she left, he started to figure in his mind how much food it would take for a young man to overwinter in a place like the Breaks. Never in his most wild imagination did Jonathon Littlestar ever think that he would be going to such lengths to protect a white man. He started to laugh again. "The Great Spirit has a sense of humor," he thought. He now had two sons, one black, the other white. The Great Spirit has a sense of humor.

But the Great Spirit had other plans for William Littlestar.

Heath knew Littlestar had Wayland hiding somewhere on the vast reservation lands. And no damned Indian would put one over on Mick Heath. Several times he sent a man on Littlestar's trail especially when the father and son would leave with what looked like a bundle of food, but always the native Americans would lose the man in some deep canyon. Once Littlestar led the man on a northern trek, almost to Canada only to return to Fort Belknap with a few antelope and mule deer. The follower returned too, haggard, hungry, and unhappy.

Then Heath began to wonder why Joe was black while his mother and father were brown. A check of Grose Ventre records found no birth certificate. No one on the reservation would talk to him about the family until one evening he found an elder who had too much to drink and wanted more.

Heath bought the old man another bottle of whiskey. He found out the Joe was taken into Littlestar's family on a trade for elk meat from a white family glad to get rid of the toddler who was the son of two black servants who had left their employers in the night never to return.

Joe Littlestar was purchased in Montana and that was against the law. One early afternoon in April, Heath along with a U.S. Marshall and several tribal deputies served warrants for Jonathon and Bellla Littlestar. The officer's guns were no match for them. Because they were a flight risk, the Littlestars were taken to Great Falls to await trial. Joe was picked up at school and taken to a holding facility somewhere in that big city.

"Now," Heath thought, "all I have to do is wait and my long-lost adopted son will make his way back here to this house." He had a man lodged in Fort Belknap to keep an eye out for the boy's return.

Carl Wayland spent a long winter in the Missouri Breaks. Between the weeks when Jonathon and Joe Littlestar brought food and other supplies, Carl explored the back country. He got to know it well and took elk, antelope, and deer whenever he needed it. He also began to wonder during those long nights and short days if life would always be like this. Memories of his mother and father began to fade. But Carl's hatred for the men who had killed them along with Mick Heath, burned with each passing day.

When the Littlestars arrived at his camp they would stay for several days. Jonathon Littlestar took the boys out and showed them how to track game, set snares, and survive undetected in the wild lands. Wayland's few pleasures in his new life were these outings with his two friends.

The days began to warm and snow melt from the high country swelled the Missouri River, overflowing its banks. Wayland's supply of beans, flour and lard were running low. The Littlestars were overdue for a visit and resupply. He went out and shot a small deer and waited. The days grew longer and warmer and still no signs of his people.

With a hunger for more than meat and a gnawing sense that something happened to the Littlestars, Wayland decided to head to Fort Belknap. He waited for a night of a hard driving rain which would erase all sign of his tracks out of his camp. He tried to not let his hunger and worry overtake his wits in avoiding detection from Heath's men.

"Joe, Joe, are you in here?" Wayland asked in the darkness of Joe's bedroom. He had found the hidden key under the rock near the back steps. All the doors to the house had been locked. Wayland had quietly opened the back door and found his way to Joe's room. The house was vacant.

There were no smells of Bella's wheat bread or of sweet, cooked meats that had always been present in this house. They have been gone awhile Wayland thought but to where and why?

He was now afraid, more afraid, and lonelier than he had ever been in his life. He could not light a lantern knowing that it would alert outsiders of his presence. Then he remembered Joe's candle next to the bed. He lit it and kept it covered with his hand. Taking it to the pantry he found a can of beans and quickly opened it. It was the first meal he had had in days.

Tomorrow night he thought, he would go to Littlestar's brother's house. Maybe they could tell me what happened. Wayland relocked the house, put the key back, and hid out in a canyon north of town.

The next night after the quarter moon had risen above the dogwoods, Wayland made his way to the home of William Littlestar. He pulled his coat tight against a biting north wind that held small flakes of spring snow. Through a side window he could see Littlestar on a chair next to a fireplace smoking a cigarette.

Wayland went to the back door and knocked. He heard Littlestar walk across the bare wood floors and approached the door.

"Who's there?" Littlestar asked.

In a whisper Wayland answered, "Mr. Littlestar, it's Carl Wayland, your brother's friend, please let me in."

Littlestar opened the door. A faint kerosene lantern shook out the darkness. "You", Littlestar said in an angry loud voice. "You ... my brother and his family are in jail because of you. If it were not for my brother, I'd turn you over to the white man and collect the $50 reward for your worthless hide."

"What, jail, me, jail?" Wayland stood cold and felt helpless looking up at the big man in front of him. "Please tell me what happened. I need to know if I can go and help them."

William Littlestar told Wayland the account of how Mick Heath managed to find a way to arrest his brother. As he spoke the young man grew angry with a simmering hatred toward the small Irishman. By the time Littlestar was through with the story Wayland knew what he had to do.

"I hope you understand I never meant to put your brother and Bella in jail," Wayland said, "and you are right, it is my fault." The two men looked at each other in the quiet of the night. "I will find some way to get them back here."

Littlestar shook his head. "It is my brother's way," he said. "Sometimes I think his heart is like that of a big buffalo who lives to protect his herd." He stepped forward and handed Wayland two $1 bills.

"Here," Littlestar said, "be on your way. Leave Fort Belknap and don't come back."

Wayland took the money, nodded a quiet thanks and made his way out.

In the darkness he crept back to Jonathon Littlestar's home. Using the key next to the stairs he again gained entry and lit the candle he found in Joe's room. With a rucksack he took what canned food he found in the pantry. There would be enough canned beans and dried corn to last him a few weeks on the trail.

Without heat the house was cold and damp and without the Littlestars it was no home at all. Wayland blew the candle out and hurried away. The house itself seemed to threaten him, telling him to go.

He found his horse and gear in the small canyon where he left them. He would travel cross country by night and hide by day.

The authorities never found out who killed Mick Heath. He had been inspecting one of his irrigation ditches on a remote part of his land. There was a bullet hole placed neatly through his chest and done with a 30-30 rifle much like the one stolen from him a year ago. But that rifle was a popular one among the plains people and the hot-headed bean farmer had made many enemies, and the debts he owed on his failing operation were considerable.

So, the law quit looking for Heath's killer especially since the sheriff's department was losing men as they enlisted to fight a new war brewing in Europe. Without Heath to press charges against the Littlestars they were soon released from jail. Joe Littlestar turned 16 in the boarding house and was by law a man, so he, too, was set free. The family returned to Fort Belknap.

# 3

# PRISON

FOR TWO YEARS WAYLAND KICKED AROUND SMALL RANCHES working odd jobs, living in barns and at times off the land. On January 1, 1918, on his 18th birthday he robbed a general store in Livingston. He was soon caught outside of town nearly dead drunk from the whiskey he bought with his ill-gotten gains.

As this was his first crime on record the court went easy on him. He got two years in the state penitentiary outside of Missoula. From his fellow inmates Wayland soon learned new trades. His prison cell mate was Josh Smith who was doing a five-year hitch for cattle stealing. Smith was caught changing brands on two stolen cows so he could sell them legally.

"Damn cattleman's association had a detective and sheriff deputy watching me," Smith explained. "I got one cow done with a brand change and was about to do the other when they came busting over the hill and nabbed me. Guess they was watchin' with a scope from a mesa."

"I think it's a hoot," Smith laughed at Wayland, "that they gave me five years for two cows while they gave you two for a robbery." He paused then continued, "but they coulda' hung me. People in these parts have never taken to cattle or horse thievin'."

Smith was 25 years old and Wayland 18. It bothered Wayland some that Smith thought it was funny that the youngster was caught so quickly.

"Boy," Smith said, "you have got a lot to learn about crime and I must say that if you do crime, you will do time. It is a matter of staying one step ahead of John Q Law that will keep you out of this place."

From the prison card sharps Wayland soon learned how to cheat at poker and get away with it. From other men he learned how to enter homes at night and steal. They told him which homes were the best marks and where people typically hide their gold, silver and other valuables and then sneak quietly away into the night. He was learning how to stay ahead of the law.

As a small young man among bigger older men, Wayland also learned how to fight and defend himself. He soon gained the respect of the other inmates with his ability to keep attacking his opponent even though his fight was lost. Wayland would come out of prison with a four-inch gash across his forehead and part of this left ear missing, the latter having been bit off in a skirmish with Billy Thompson.

Other than that Wayland didn't mind doing his prison sentence; he thought it was partial payment for his killing Heath. He also had a softer warmer place to sleep and three regular meals a day. Being a model prisoner, unfortunately caused him to get an early release after a year and a half.

A few days before getting out Josh Smith asked a favor of Wayland.

"I've got a sister in Bozeman," he said. "Could you go see her and give her this packet with ten dollars and a letter? The letter explains a few things about my life and my apology to my folks for being here. You see they disowned me for disgracin' the family's good name." Smith added that there was a lumbermill in Bozeman where he might find work, seems they are always "short of men."

With a handshake Wayland departed his friend and after walking out of the pen headed west to Bozeman. However first he stopped off in Butte for several nights, taking enough money at poker from drunken miners to keep going for another few weeks. He hitched a ride on a logging wagon sharing whiskey with the driver on the long road east.

The Smith family was tending a garden when the

logging truck pulled up and let Wayland off. With the address and description of the house, he knew he was at the right place.

"I'm looking for a Miss Laura Smith," he said, approaching a young woman who was attacking weeds with a broad hoe. An older woman in her late forties stepped up quickly and asked "Who's calling?"

Wayland took off his hat and said "Pardon me ma'am. I'm Carl Wayland and I've got a letter here from Josh Smith for his sister Miss Laura Smith."

"If you know Josh you must be a convict", the woman said in a high-pitched voice. She stood about six foot tall, half a head over Wayland. With a stern hard-set brow over her eyes and broad hoe in her hand, Wayland step back a bit nervous.

"Beg pardon ma'am, but yes Josh and I were friends in Missoula."

The woman wrinkled her face in disgust, "If you're a friend of his I'd be pleased if you just be on your way and don't come back."

The young woman dropped here hoe and came forward. "Mom, it is my letter, and I am going to take it."

She accepted the packet from Wayland and with a curt "you," put it inside her dress and went back to her chores.

"Please ma'am," Wayland said to the matron, "could you tell me where I could find a place to sleep for the night?"

The older woman turned her back to the garden and

without turning said aloud, "Applebee's place four blocks west and one south."

Wayland replaced his hat and walked away.

A few hours later at the boarding house Wayland received a visitor.

"Hi," she said extending a hand, "I'm Laura Smith, can we talk?"

Wayland looked at the young woman in front of him. She no longer wore the long work dress or had on the butterfly hat that covered what was to him one of the most beautiful faces he had ever laid eyes on. He stood in the entry way a bit dumbfounded.

With the summer evening ending and the sun setting in the Montana sky, Laura Smith looked up and down the street and then pushed her way past Wayland into the house.

"Sorry" she said, "I can't afford to have any of my neighbors or friends see me in a place like this. Well, if it ever gets back to mama that I came she'd have daddy take a switch to me."

That possible scene hit Wayland as funny and broke him out of his love at first site stupor. He laughed, saying, "Aren't you a bit old to be wailed on by your father?"

"You don't know daddy," she said. "He used to give the willow to Josh until Josh one night had enough and broke all the switches and left. That was six years ago and he ain't been back since."

Wayland was about to speak when Smith quickly broke in again, "Mr. Wayland, you just have to tell me all you can about Josh. I have missed him so. He was my only refuge from my father and mother's wrath. Josh's letter says he is well, but he'd lie to make me feel better. He's doing okay in that awful place isn't he"?

Wayland tried to speak again, "Yes he is doing..."

"You wouldn't be like Josh and lie to me too would you, I mean just to protect my feelings?  Josh didn't tell you what to say did he?" Smith asked.

A boarder stuck his head out of a side room annoyed at the loud conversation going on in the hallway.

Wayland gently steered Smith into his room and closed the door.

She looked nervously about and sat down at a small table. Wayland took the other chair.

"Miss Smith," Wayland said, "Let me..."

"Please call me Laura, my friends do, and any friend of Josh's is a friend of mine," she said. "Can I call you Carl?  Now you were saying about my brother..."

Carl took a deep breath. It had been a while since he had to deal with a woman, and this one had the energy of a Chinook wind.

"Your brother is doing fine," Wayland said, "Oh, he like me, has been in a couple of scrapes with other inmates but he has held his own. He told me a great deal about you, and I can see he was right about how pretty you are."

"Why, why, thank you Mr. Wayland, I mean Carl, that is nice of you to say," Laura said. "Josh said in his letter that you and he were good friends and how you stood up for him once with the guards. Fact is it was his idea to have me come and see you. My look at the time I really should be going I told mama I was only going for a short walk, and ..."

This time Wayland jumped in. "Laura, I'm going to try and get a job here in Bozeman." He took her hand and held it with both of his. "Would you mind if I saw you again?"

She looked down at her hand inside Wayland's. Something deep inside, an inexplicable feeling began to stir, and she let it take hold of her. Maybe she thought, this is what Josh wanted us to do all along.

"Yes," she said, "but we cannot let mama or daddy find out." This was exciting for her, a new adventure that she hoped would eventually take her far from Bozeman, far from her parents and far from that stupid damn garden. She also hoped it would reunite her with her brother.

"Carl, I have a trusted friend, Mary Lou Obernocki, and she can drop off and pick up messages here at the boarding house or wherever you might end up."

To Wayland's surprise Laura stood up, came over to

his chair and kissed him on the lips.

"That's the first time I've ever done that," she said with a devil made smile. "And it won't be the last." She left Carl Wayland frozen to his chair. No convict in the pen had ever hit him that hard.

# 4

# LEAVING BOZEMAN

WHEN LAURA SMITH WAS TWO MONTHS WITH CHILD, SHE confided the fact to Wayland. He decided it was time for them to move on anyway since some of the gambling saloons were soon on to him and his overly lucky card playing. Most of the old-time gamblers wouldn't play with him anymore. Wayland had saved enough money from working the sawmill, which he hated, and gambling, which he loved, to buy him a used truck.

He and Laura planned their getaway. One Sunday morning in October she told her parents she was too sick to go to church. Her father warned that after church he would bring the parish doctor by the house. If she was faking the illness, he would find out and she would get the willow. No, Laura thought to herself, I would not get the damn willow this time or ever again. After her parents left the house Laura grabbed her pre-bundled carpet bag and made her way to Wayland's truck down the street. She left a note that said simply "Goodbye, don't come looking."

Under her new hat and wrap no one recognized the young woman who tossed a bag into the back of a beat-up truck, hopped into the passenger's seat and with an eager yell said, "Go!"

At the Missoula prison they found out that Josh had been framed for beating up a guard. Despite the fact he was nowhere near the guard during the beating, Josh was accused by other inmates. He got three more years added to his sentence. He had been two months away from an early release.

Angry and bitter, he lashed out at two inmates during lunch one afternoon and almost slit a man's throat with a sharpened spoon. He was in solitary confinement when Wayland and his sister arrived. No visitors, no letters, no outside contact whatsoever. The guards wouldn't even let Josh know that Wayland or his sister had come to see him.

Wayland wasn't sure what to do now. The only plan he had was to pick up Josh so the three of them could make a life somewhere in Montana. It was Laura's idea to head up to Fort Belknap. "We have got to get away soon from Missoula," she told Wayland. "If daddy comes a looking for me, he'll know I have come to see Josh."

Wayland agreed. Even though he could legally marry Laura he did not want to put up with an angry father.

The two and almost three headed north. Across wind cratered gravel and sand roads they found their way to Fort Belknap. They arrived the same time a Canadian blizzard swept in from the northwest. The old truck barely made it through the snow into the Littlestar's driveway.

After knocking on the door, it was opened by Bella who quickly took them in. The half-frozen Laura was put by the fire and given hot elk stew.

Carl got a big hug from Bella. "We thought you were dead," she said. "We had heard about that Mick Heath." She stopped and looked into Carl's eyes, and she knew. Carl stood before her, and he knew that she knew, and he nodded.

"That, that was many old summers ago and all is forgotten, all is now forgiven," she said.

"And my Littlestars had to go all the way to the Rocky Mountains this year for elk," Bella said, explaining the absence of Jonathon and Joe. She added: "Since the white men have come back from that war in the white mans' old country, they have taken much of the game around the reservation lands. We complain to the agents about it, but it does no good. Sometimes they just shoot deer and let them lay to rot."

Bella looked out the window. "I had hoped the boys

would be back by now, but this snow will hold them up." She looked again at Wayland, saying "You remember that Joe was a big boy; well, he has grown into a bigger man, almost twice the size of his father."

At that Wayland laughed. Jonathon Littlestar was 6 foot two inches and weighed 265 pounds. Twice that size was more than he could imagine.

Bella laughed, too. "I think it was all that elk stew I fed him," she said, and she looked at Laura by the stove. "When is the baby due?" she asked.

"Sometime in the spring," Laura said surprised by the question, thinking she wasn't quite showing yet especially under the coat and blanket. "I'm not exactly sure."

"It will be a boy," Bella said. "It is the way you are holding the bowl of elk stew."

Laura was not sure how to take that announcement, but she believed her.

Six months later Bella helped deliver Laura's baby, a boy. He weighed five and half pounds and was, according to Bella, "too early for this world."

Out of Laura's ear shot, Bella told Carl the baby might die unless they could get the new lungs breathing properly. Bella called in a tribal mid-wife. After talking to her, Bella told Carl that the baby had to be put in a steaming room with boiled mountain cedar boughs.

Carl told Bella to do whatever it took to keep his son alive. Jonathan quickly built a special sweat lodge big enough for two people. Bella was the only one allowed inside to help Laura. After 35 days, Bella emerged from the lodge with a dark-haired boy now flush with a bit more color.

She gave the boy to Carl. He took the baby into his arms but oddly felt nothing. He had wondered what this moment would be like and tried to conjure up a tender emotion, but it would not come. The baby, asleep, seemed foreign to him. "What have I done," he thought, "bringing a kid into this damn world."

Wayland smiled at Bella. "Thank you," he said. "I've decided to name him John after my adopted father here but from now on I will call him Jack." He handed the baby back to Bella.

"To ensure everything is all right we will keep Jack and Laura in the lodge for two more weeks," Bella said. She added that Laura had a hard delivery and was still in some pain and is weak.

"Can I see her now?" Wayland asked.

"Yes," Bella said, "but only for a few minutes."

Wayland went inside the small hut. One candle lit the small room. The air was warm and heavy with moisture and the scent of pine.

"Carl", Laura cried out, "is that you?"

"Laura, I'm here," he said. "Bella has the baby and will bring him to you in a few minutes. I can't stay long. He is a fine-looking boy, Laura. You did well. I named him Jack after Jonathon Littlestar. I owe so much to these people. You understand, don't you?"

"Yes," Laura said, "and without Bella I and the baby would have died. Jack is a good name. I worry so, Carl, the baby is so small."

"Bella will take care of you and him. She knows what to do. Well, well, I have to go know. In a few weeks we will be a family again. Good by Laura," Wayland said, and kissed her gently on the forehead and left. Bella took the baby inside.

"Where are you going?" Jonathon asked Wayland, who was heading for his truck.

"There is something I need to do," Wayland said. "I'll be back soon."

"Your wife and child need you here," Littlestar said.

Over his shoulder Wayland said, "I'll be back." Then he got into his truck and drove west.

In Livingston, Montana, Carl Wayland used up all his hidden gambling money at the Wild Mare whore house. In two weeks, he did not have a sober moment. Finally, dead broke with only enough money for gas to get him back to Fort Belknap, he headed for home.

All the way back he thought of Laura and Jack. He also wanted another drink, but Laura and Jack would have to come first.

When he arrived at the Littlestars, he got out of the truck and started walking toward the sweat lodge. Part way across the drive he was met by Jonathon.

"Wait," he yelled, and took one look at Wayland, stepped back, and hit him hard across the face with a fisted right.

Wayland went into the dust. He sat, unable to get up and cried. "Why Jonathon, why?"

"Because I'm your father," Littlestar said, "and that is what father's do."

Wayland did not have another drink for two years. When he did it was the beginning of the end.

# 5

# THE SECOND SON

THAT BEGINNING CAME WITH THE BIRTH OF HIS SECOND son. It would be that son who would plunge a knife into Wayland's chest 16 years later.

This son was born with blonde hair and blue eyes and weighed eight pounds and was an easy delivery. Unlike his brother, this boy was strong and healthy right out of the womb.

But Wayland looked at Laura and her black hair. He looked at Jack and his black hair and with his own dark hair he began to wonder if Laura had been untrue to him. It could be, he thought, that this baby had another father.

What Wayland didn't know, and what Laura tried unsuccessfully to tell him, was that her father was blond and had blue eyes. Josh, her brother, was also blond.

"Damn you, bitch. I want to know who the father is," Wayland demanded.

"It's yours, I swear it's yours, oh God, Carl," Laura pleaded. "I love you. I wouldn't have been with anyone else. I swear, oh, Carl, you have to believe me."

Wayland answered: "All the time I was a gone on the elk and deer hunts with Joe and Jonathon and you here all alone. I don't know what to believe. I am glad we moved out of Fort Belknap six months ago so Jonathon can't see what I am about to do."

With that he left Laura with the two boys. He made his way down to a once familiar whore house in Livingston, the city where they now lived since leaving the Littlestar home. He bought a bottle of whiskey, checked in with the madam and found a room upstairs.

In the morning, still drunk, he returned home and beat Laura near senseless. With the baby crying, Wayland picked up the newborn from its crib and gave it to Laura.

"Here," he said, "feed this little bastard." He then took Jack and left for breakfast downtown.

Despite Laura's constant reassurances, Wayland, especially while drinking, could not escape the thought that this blond-haired boy was sired by someone else.

Laura named the boy Orton after her brother's middle name, which she was always fond of. Wayland didn't care what she called him. He was only interested in Jack whom he finally began to show some affection while ignoring his new son.

When Orton was four years old and Jack was six, the former stood a foot taller than his brother. This only infuriated Wayland who took every opportunity to trip the youngster as he toddled across the floor. He also held back food from Orton and tried to force feed Jack hoping to get him to grow bigger. While Orton had a voracious appetite, scrawny Jack ate little. Laura, often on the sly, made sure Orton had enough to eat.

Growing up, Orton did not understand why his father favored his older brother. It was just the way it was for him. One Saturday when he was 12 years old, he wandered into Harshaw's Car Repair shop. He was amazed by the men working with tools fixing trucks, cars, and the occasional buggy of which a few were still around.

"Hey kid," said a voice, "hand me that number two wrench on the shelf." The man's legs stuck out from under the truck and a hand was held out for the unseen tool.

Orton didn't know a number two from three but another man with a tire under his arm pointed it out and Orton delivered. "Thanks," the man said.

"What're you doin' under there?" Orton asked, sitting on his feet, and trying hard to make sense of this work.

"Trying to fix this damn leak in this transmission and I hope I don't have to take it apart to do it," said the man.

The man came out from under the truck and looked at the wide-eyed young man in frayed brown corduroy pants.

"You like cars and truck?" the man asked.

Orton looked up at the big man whose face and arms needed an oil change. With his whole body, Orton nodded yes.

Bill Harshaw grabbed a piece of gunny sack and cleaned the wet oil from his hands and neck. He then shook the top knot of Orton's head and said, "Okay kid, I need a gofer boy, so I'll teach you the tools. Would you like that?"

Again, with a full body nod, Orton answered yes. "Can we do it today?" he asked. "My dad and brother are out fishing, and I want to learn about cars."

Harshaw laughed at the youth's eagerness. "Sure kid, "he said, "I can't pay you much but..."

Orton cut him off. "I don't care about the money. I only want to learn about the cars."

While Wayland and Jack were gone on hunting and fishing trips, Orton poured his energy into taking apart engines, transmissions, and carburetors. He also learned about knife fighting.

One Friday evening when Harshaw was out on a service call and Orton was alone in the shop, a man came in for his car.

"Where's the '32 Ford?" he asked.

"Behind the shop," Orton said cranking on a valve under a truck's hood. The man returned a few minutes later.

"I want the keys," he demanded.

"Can't give you those," Orton said, "Only Harshaw can do that, and he will be back soon."

The man grabbed Orton's shirt by the back of the collar and pulled him backward off the truck, banging his head on the way out. In a split second the man had a long blade knife at Orton's throat.

"Listen kid, you will get me those keys right now or this will be the last truck you ever work on," the man said.

Trembling in fear to the point where he could only whisper, Orton said, "Sure Mister, I'll get them for you."

The garage was then filled with a booming roar. "Okonski!" It was Harshaw. "Okonski, maybe you had better deal with me instead of my partner."

The man took the knife off Orton's throat and turned to greet Harshaw. He took a few steps away from Orton.

"I came here to get my car," Okonski said. "And I ain't leavin' without it."

"You can have it when you pay me the forty dollars for the fix," Harshaw replied.

Okonski, a foot taller and fifty pounds heavier, took a lunge with the knife toward Harshaw's chest.

In a blink of Orton's eye, Harshaw had the knife out of Okonski's hand and had put the big man faced down into the greasy dirt. "I now have your knife and your car Okonski. If you want me to take your life too, I can do that. I have a witness that will vouch that you attacked me first. So, what'll it be?"

Now in a pig squeal voice Okonski said, "Okay, I'll pay you. Let me up. The money is in my wallet."

Okonski got up. He took forty dollars out of his billfold, the last money he had left, and gave it to Harshaw. Harshaw took the car keys from his back pocket and gave them to Okonski.

"Don't ever come back here again," Harshaw said.

"What about that knife?" Okonski asked.

Harshaw smiled. "That'll be another forty dollars."

With an angry head shake, Okonski went out the back of the shop, got into his car, and quickly drove away.

Harshaw walked over to Orton and handed him the knife. "Here kid, I think you earned this."

Still trembling, Orton took the knife that had a deer antler for a handle. It was obviously well crafted.

"How did you do that, Mr. Harshaw? How did you take the knife from that big guy?" Orton asked.

"Oh that, that was something my dad taught me years ago. He was in the army and .... hey.... do you want me to show you how to do that, too?" Harshaw asked.

Orton smiled and with his whole body nodded yes, adding: "But the next time somebody comes into this shop I won't have my back to them."

Where Jack patterned his life after his father, Orton took after Harshaw with whom he was now spending more of his time. Harshaw neither smoked nor drank and tended toward fairness in his business dealings. Orton also enjoyed the shop owner's sense of humor.

One early evening two young girls came to the shop looking for the blond handsome mechanic. Harshaw met them and asked what they needed. When he found out, he said Orton was out back fixing his Johnson rod but would be back in a few minutes.

When Orton came out, he recognized the girls from school and said "Hello."

"Mr. Harshaw said you were out back fixing your Johnson rod," one of the girls said sweetly.

"Oh no," Orton said without thinking. "I was just in the outhouse." Orton's face began to turn red. Harshaw had got him again. Last Saturday Harshaw had sent Orton to the parts store to pick up a pair of muffler bearings. Those and Johnson rods do not exist but refer to something else.

In the office he could hear Harshaw laughing. He came out, asking "Did you fix that Johnson rod?"

Orton's nervously nodded yes but began to laugh with Harshaw. The girls looked from one man to the other. "What's so funny?" they asked.

Orton took the kidding as a sign of affection. Harshaw didn't joke with just anyone -- only the people he cared about.

One afternoon Harshaw's wife stopped in to meet this new employee her husband had been talking about. The small round-faced woman took an immediate liking to this modest well-mannered youth. Along with his good-natured way of talking, she also noticed how skinny Orton was.

The next day in Harshaw's lunch box he found a piece of Shepherd's pie with a note that said, "Orton." That afternoon when he finished his lunch, Orton ran out to the back alley where wild prairie roses were growing. He had Harshaw put two of them in the empty lunch box with a thank-you note. Orton ate out of that lunch box with Harshaw from that day forward.

Orton's own mother lived in a state of misery. The once petite young woman with a face of fair complexion was now pale and pock marked. Age lines were beginning to map her eyes along with a shallow darkness that looked out from them. At home alone she took to drinking whiskey and smoking cigarettes, both of which seemed to be in endless supply in the house. Wayland rarely spoke to her and when he did it was to complain about his dinner which he demanded ready when he came home from work. The other time he spoke to Laura is when he told her to "shut up and butt out" when he disciplined Orton with hand slaps for some minor issue. Occasionally he beat the two of them. Jack was left untouched.

The night Orton got his worst beating is when

Wayland came home and found no dinner on the table. Under a knife stuck in a loaf of stale bread was a note from Laura that said, "Goodbye, don't come looking for me."

Orton had just walked in the door from Harshaw's when Wayland took out his rage on the young man. Wayland's fists flew and Orton cried. He cried not so much from the pain of the beating but from the note he found on the floor as he lay in a heap. Wayland sat at the table and emptied a bottle of Old Crow. Orton, in the darkness of his corner, thought about his mother. In a way he was glad she'd escaped Wayland's meanness. Gone, however, was his home's last refuge of love. So, Orton sobbed, his father laughed, and a son's hatred for a father sprouted from a seed planted long ago.

Orton never spoke to Harshaw about his home life. He explained the bruises on his face as brotherly jousts, even though Jack kept his distance from a younger brother twice his size. Wayland needed the money Orton made to help pay for house expenses. Orton also worked on Wayland's truck and kept it running, a vehicle that needed constant repair.

About two years after Laura left, Wayland came home and told the boys to pack of few of their belongings. A gambling debt had put the house up for foreclosure. Wayland lost his job at the lumber company. His reputation established in Livingston proved him unhireable, anyplace. He told the boys they were headed to Fort Belknap, but what he didn't tell the boys was his plan to make them rich.

Wayland's job trucking for Livingston Lumber often took him into Great Falls, a sprawling Montana city on the Missouri River. It was the wheat and smelting ore hub of the state.

# 6

# SUE ANN YANCY

ON A DELIVERY OF LUMBER TO A NEW ADDITION TO THE FIRST National Bank downtown on Central Avenue, Wayland had stood by his truck as men unloaded his freight. Looking across the street he saw a young lady in white lace and a frilly dress at the entry to a soda shop.

"Who's that?" Wayland asked the crews foreman standing by.

"Oh, that missy", the foreman said in a Scottish accent nodding in the direction of the shop, "that's your Sue Ann Yancy and a wild one she is. Her father is Lambert Yancy the owner of this bank and part of the railroad. Miss Yancy is the apple of her dear dod's eye."

Wayland watched as the girl met her friends at the shop's doorway. They talked a few minutes and then laughing together went inside.

As he drove back to Livingston Wayland saw it clear how he would kidnap the fancy of her "dod's" eye for which he would pay handsomely for her return. He knew he could hide her in the Missouri Breaks, make his money and then high tail it to Mexico. Down there he and the boys could buy a ranch and live like kings. Wayland smiled at the thought of all those brown skin chiquitas that would be at his pleasure.

A few months later, after his house had been taken by the sheriff, he and his sons were on their way to Fort Belknap. Orton drove, Jack sat in the middle and Wayland took the more comfortable passenger seat. As they headed north, Wayland laid out his plans to the boys.

"Orton," he said, "when the time comes, you'll be the one who goes into the soda shop and gets that Miss Yancy girl." He showed Orton a photo of Sue Ann Yancy and her father at a Great Falls gala. "She is usually wearing white or pale blue. Go in and ask for her and tell her that her father fell ill, is in the hospital and is asking for her. I'm sure she will go with you. If she asks where her other driver is, tell her he is on another call and that you were the only one available. Got it?"

Orton didn't like the idea but nodded "Yes."

"Jack," Wayland said, "you will be the look out on the street. Before Orton goes into the shop you give him a hand wave that things are all clear. If any police are in the area keep your hands down. When Orton gets the girl, he'll head toward the hospital and pick you up on the corner. After you get in put a gun to her head and say that if she screams, you'll kill her."

The eighteen-year-old Jack smiled and winked at his dad. He spit a wad of tobacco into a tin cup he was holding. Wayland grabbed the cup and did same.

Wayland continued: "I've a friend named George who has a garage and horse corral at the entry to the Breaks. We'll hide the truck in the garage and take a horse and buggy rig into the back country. I also bought another horse in case we need it. If John Law comes looking, they will have to come on horseback, and we will have time to escape east."

As Orton listened, he took in how his dad had worked on this idea. As a member of this trio, he was committing himself to being an outlaw, a thought he did not exactly cherish.

"Dad," Orton asked, "no harm is going to come to the girl, right?"

Wayland mock surprised, "Of course not. Once we get the ransom money, we'll drop her off at a way station in the middle of the night and we'll head south. The law won't have a clue as to who did it. By the two or three days it takes them to get organized we'll be drinking tequila in Cananea."

"Cananea?" Orton asked. "Where in Mexico is that. How did you pick that place?"

"It's about 100 miles south of the border from

Juarez," Wayland replied. "Two of my old convict pals are down there now."

They had only been gone from Livingston for three hours and already Orton was missing the Harshaws and a young girl he'd been seeing for a few months. He said his good-byes yesterday. With Harshaw, the parting was the worst. He told Harshaw that he'd be back in a couple of months-- that this move was only temporary. Harshaw, who knew Wayland, shook his head in disgust and then shook Orton's hand good-bye. "If you ever need a job as a mechanic," he said, "there is one waiting for you here. Or if you need anything...." Orton's eyes had filled with tears as he turned and walked away.

The road into the Breaks was one of sand and rock. Twice they had to stop and repair blown tires. Soon after passing a slit between two rock outcroppings, they came to an open area that had a small shack, a garage, and corral with three horses.

"We're almost home boys," Wayland announced. "We will stay at George's here tonight and head into the Breaks in the morning. Jack, you grab the bed rolls. Orton put the truck in the garage and make sure to shut the door."

Wayland grabbed a bottle of whiskey from a box in the truck bed. "Orton, grab this box on the way in. I'm getting a might hungry."

The box contained canned beans, eggs, and bacon.

As Jack took the bedrolls, he said to Orton, "I can't wait to be out of this damn Montana cold weather. Just think Orton, in three weeks we'll be laying under a warm Mexico sun maybe next to one of them sweet Mexican gals."

"We won't ever be able to come back into the United States, "Orton said. "She will have a description of us, and you and I will be wanted for kidnapping. That could be a hanging offense. She won't be able to tell the law about dad because she'll be bound and gagged by the time we get her up here."

"Who gives a damn if we never come back here again?" Jack yelled. "I hate this God forsaken rocky country where the wind blows forever, and you can't find a damn job that pays anything. Montana can go to hell all's I care."

It was mid-September, and a cool wind was blowing in from the north. The sun was quickly dropping in the hills of the Breaks and the night was cold. Orton thought about the warmth of Harshaw's shop where in winter a big potbellied stove kept the place bearable in the coldest of temps. What little he learned about Mexico was that it had plenty of cactus, sand, and snakes. Orton laughed to himself: "Our southern neighbor was soon to get three more of the latter."

That night on the floor of the two-room shack, Orton lay awake. He hated his dad once more for losing the house in Livingston and now with this plan to take an innocent girl from her father for the few dollars it would bring.

Wayland was asleep in the one bedroom. He slept a drunk's sleep, snoring loudly and dead to the world. Around him Orton could hear mice scurrying about the floor which reeked of old blood from processed game and horse dung brought in on the owner's boots. His brother Jack slept sound, too, having found the last few swallows of the bottle Wayland left behind.

Orton knew they would have to take the girl soon. Winter closes in fast in these parts. In a month an early snowstorm could prevent their escape south. Orton was nervous. He thought about what could go wrong with his dad's plan. Miss Yancy might have a bodyguard close by,the old truck could break down on their way out of town or Jack might miss seeing a police officer and not signal Orton in time.

Then it occurred to Orton that he didn't have to participate in this crime. He could bide his time and wait for the chance to leave his dad and Jack. He was old enough, now being 16, to go it alone. He could not go back to Harshaws because that would be the first place his father would look for him. But he could go east, maybe Detroit, Michigan. Harshaw had told him that was the place where they built all the cars and trucks Orton worked on. With his experience, he knew he could get a job there. With that in mind, the young mechanic drifted off to sleep, a mouse nibbling at the leather on his boot.

The next morning the trio got up, made a breakfast of eggs and bacon, and later loaded their gear and supplies in the old wagon. As Jack was hitching up the horse to the wagon Wayland mounted his horse.

"I'll go on ahead and check the trail," he said. "Jack, you drive the buggy in as you know the way. Your brother's never been back here. And Jack," Wayland looked directly into his elder son's face, "keep away from that damn case of whiskey until we get to the Canyon Camp."

Jack nodded a sorry agreement. Orton climbed up next to Jack and they were on their way.

Orton had never seen the Breaks this side of the Missouri. It was a land of rugged hills, flat topped mesas, and high buttes carved out long ago by the wanderings of an untamed river. It hadn't rained for a while so most of the bottom lands were dry and easily passable. From atop one mesa, Orton could see the Missouri flowing in all its quiet splendor. He took note of the white sandstone cliffs laden with layers of red river clay born centuries ago and hardened by the pressures of a mountain range long since eroded by time.

Orton found himself trying to work out the details of how he would leave his brother and dad. He was interrupted in his thoughts by Jack.

"I've a feeling you don't think much of dad's plan to make us all rich do ya?" Jack asked. Before Orton could reply Jack went on. "Dad's even wonderin' whether you up to doing this job. Just to let you know, he and I will be keepin' an eye on you. We need you to keep that old truck runnin'. Dad gave me his extra gun so don't go making any other plan."

"C'mon now Jack," Orton said, "I'm with you. Where the hell would I go anyway?"

"I dunno," Jack replied, "but we are keeping you in our sights anyways."

Three hours later they arrived at the Canyon Camp. This was a small two room cabin a hundred yards from the river. Inside was a bunk bed built into the wall, a metal wood stove, and a table with three chairs. A side door led to a small bedroom with a single bed and an oil lamp on a small table. Toward the river Orton could see a makeshift raft on a high bank roped to a cottonwood tree. Driftwood from spring and storm runoff littered the shoreline.

A horse trail through a back canyon wall provided an escape to the east. That would be the one they'd use if the law came in from the west. Not that they would get far with four people riding two horses. Or, Orton thought, would it be two men on two horses?

Behind the cabin rose a high butte, a flat tabletop of rock. Orton guessed that someone up there could see for miles in any direction. Wayland had picked this place well.

"Dad and I have been coming here for years," Jack said. "See that there set of deer horns?" He pointed to a wide rack of antlers hanging from the center ridge pole coming out of the cabin. "I got that one two years ago. Dad let me get drunk with him for the first time for shooting that big bastard. We sure had a night that night, by God."

In a way Orton envied his brother and the closeness shared between a father and a son. He never understood why his father mistreated him. Because of that he'd never felt part of this family, especially since his mother ran off. Damn, he thought, why didn't she take me with her?

The next day Wayland went through the plan again with Jack and Orton. When he finished the boys gave their approval that they understood what they each had to do.

"Good," Wayland said. "Today is Wednesday and on Friday, you two will leave for Great Falls early in the morning. The Yancy girl will be with her friends mid-morning on Saturday and that is when you take her. After you bring the girl here, I'll go into Fort Belknap and send a telegram with our demands. I'll spend the night there and wait for a reply. Am hoping by next week at this time we'll be on our way south.

Orton looked at the guns hanging from the hips on

Jack and his dad. South, he thought. I guess I am going south. Again, he resented his father for putting him in this position. He'd seen the poster of criminals wanted by the FBI in the Livingston post office. He figured his might be with them someday. What would Harshaw think of that?

He had two days. Orton thought of the raft by the river, he thought of grabbing Jack's gun, tying the two of them up and making his way east. But he knew he couldn't escape. He was as much a hostage here as Miss Sue Ann Yancy would be in a few days. He also knew that his father wouldn't hesitate to kill him if he did not do as he was told.

# 7

# THE HOSTAGE

ORTON FELT A BIT RIDICULOUS. HIS DAD HAD FOUND HIM A flat-topped drivers hat with a short brim. The hat, along with a long brown leather coat, made him look like other chauffeurs he'd seen in photos and magazines. The coat smelled of cigar smoke. Orton could not have guessed where Wayland had picked it up.

He knew that get-up would attract attention, and it did the moment he walked into Henson's Drug and Soda Shop. The place was full of late morning patrons talking loudly of another war brewing in Europe. People watched him as he walked in, eyes shifting onto his hat and coat. He ignored them. From the description and photo Wayland had provided, Orton saw Sue Ann Yancy with three of her friends at a table near the serving bar. Teacups and cakes sat in front of each of them.

Sweat trickled down the back of his neck. "Miss Sue Ann Yancy?" he inquired aloud, walking up to the table.

The other girls became quiet. Sue Ann Yancy spoke – "And to whom do I have this pleasure?" she asked, giggling with big brown eye lashes battering at Orton.

Orton got closer and in a toned-down voice said, "Miss Yancy, your father has taken suddenly ill. It could be a stroke and he's in a bad way. I'm to take you to the hospital. Your father has been asking for you."

The girl looked stunned. "Daddy, daddy, sick, hospital, no, no, it cannot be," she said. She looked about the room. "Where is Donald our carriage driver? Why isn't he here?"

"Mr. Donald is at the hospital," Orton said, "Please we must leave now."

Yancy looked at her friends at the table. "I've got to go," she said. She picked up her small purse, got out of the chair, and followed Orton out of the shop.

On the street she looked for the carriage car. Orton diverted her to a shabby truck that had a recent polish.

"We're going in that?" Yancy asked loudly, looking from the truck to Orton and back.

Almost in a panic Orton said, "It's all the bank could spare at the last minute. Get in. Your father needs you."

Used to being told, Sue Ann Yancy obeyed Orton's command. Orton opened the passenger door, and she got in, frightened, worried and in tears.

Orton quickly got in the driver's seat, started the engine, and drove three blocks toward the hospital. At the corner of second and main he pulled over. Jack jumped in next to the girl.

"What, who is this?" she screamed, "What—?"

Jack pulled out his gun making sure she saw it between them and said, "One more word girl and this gun will blow a hole in you so be quiet. Now get your head down."

Sue Ann Yancy was too frightened to move. She began to cry. Jack forced he head down with a heavy hand behind her neck. She screamed. Jack yelled, "Shut up you little bitch."

Orton turned up third street and began to make his way out of town. "Take it easy on her will ya?", he said." Don't hurt her."

By now Yancy, her head and shoulders pushed almost below the dashboard, was sobbing uncontrollably. Jack kept a strong hand on her back and looked out the truck window as if he were on a Sunday drive. Occasionally, at stop signs, he paused to wave and smile as people crossed the street.

When they broke free of the city onto the flat plains, Jack had had enough. He pulled the girl's head back and wrapped a dirty bandana around her mouth with a knot securing it behind her head. "There," he said, "that'll shut you for a while." He also put a bandana around the girl's eyes.

Sue Ann Yancy rocked back and forth. Jack laughed. Orton shook his head and looked at the girl. "Can you breathe, okay?" he asked her. With grimaced fear showing on her face and tears coming out from under the wrap, she nodded yes and continued her rocking motion.

Why? Orton thought, why damnit are we putting this poor girl through all this? He knew the answer was part of his dad's plan. Jack had the gun. Orton drove on.

As the sun began to settle on the Missouri river bottom, Orton pulled the truck into George's camp. Wayland met them in the drive. When Jack got the girl out of the truck and took her into the shack, Wayland turned to Orton.

"Where in the hell have you been?" he asked loudly.

Orton looked into his dad's angry eyes.

"We had a flat tire and we had to get gas in Belt," Orton said, "and I think one of the cylinders is starting to knock. I couldn't push the truck past 40."

Orton lied about the engine trouble. Jack and his dad couldn't tell engine problems from its sound, and Orton hoped it might divert their plans. It didn't.

"Well," said Wayland, "we need the truck in top shape if it's to take us down to Mexico. You might have to stay here and work on it while Jack and I take the girl into the break's camp."

Orton realized he couldn't leave the girl in his dad's and Jack's company. He feared what they might do to her.

"Let me take a look again at the engine whilst I still have some daylight," Orton said, "I may be able to adjust the lifter. Shouldn't take me long."

With that Orton got under the hood with a few tools and did some minor adjustments.

"That should do it," he said, and climbed into the truck and started the engine. Stepping hard on the gas he let the engine roar a bit.

Wayland smiled. "Put the truck in the garage," he said. "We'll spend the night here. You boys will take the girl to the hideout camp tomorrow while I go into Fort Belknap and telegraph her father with our demands."

After he put the truck away, Orton went into the shack. Sue Ann Yancy sat at the table with her legs tied to the chair. The bandana had been taken off her mouth. The blindfold remained. In front of her was a plate full of beans.

Jack looked at Orton and then the girl.

"She won't eat," Jack said, "and she won't say a thing either."

Orton knew the girl was in a state of shock. Her life of ease and comfort was now reduced to a fate for which she had no control. There were too many miles of tears and road between her and her father. She sat numb, unfeeling, alone. Despair set in.

"Where is she going to sleep?" Orton asked. Jack grinned.

Wayland said, "We'll tie her in the bed in the other room and I'll sleep on the floor next to her so she can't escape. You two find your bed rolls and sleep on the floor in here."

"You aren't going to harm her are you dad?" Orton asked.

Again, with fake surprise Wayland answered, "What? Do you think I'm going to harm the treasure that'll bring us the money we need to start a life in Mexico?" He then added, "It's none of your damn business anyway."

At the word "Mexico," Sue Ann Yancy turned her head toward Wayland, and Wayland knew he shouldn't have spoken. Orton caught it, too. That seals her fate, Orton thought. Wayland's not going to let her go and tell the law where to look for her abductors. Federal lawmen couldn't cross the border, but it wouldn't stop private detectives hired by the bank president.

Wayland and Jack took the girl into the bedroom and tied her hands and feet to the bed posts.

Wayland spread his bed roll on the floor next to her.

"Maybe we should keep the door open to make sure she gets enough good air," Orton suggested.

"Get," Wayland said and shut the bedroom door when the two boys left. He turned the oil lamp down low and looked at the girl on the bed. Much prettier than any of the whores he knew in Livingston, he thought, but not much younger. He thought, too, of how his plan was working just as he believed it would. He looked again at the girl on the bed. Maybe even better. He blew out the oil lamp.

The next morning Wayland was up early and in a good mood. "Jack, Orton," he said aloud, "get the hell up." Wayland got a fire going and made coffee. He told Jack to dump some bacon grease into his cooked oats. "Make sure you make enough for our guest, too," he said.

While Wayland was having his coffee, Orton looked in on Miss Yancy laying on the straw tick mattress. Her breathing was slow with long pauses. Her once golden ringlets of hair now lay in a pleated mess on the dirty pillow. In her mouth and fastened to the back of her head was a bandana, the same kind dirty cloth that still covered her eyes. Somehow her dress did not look right.

"Shut that door and leave her be," Wayland said to Orton, "After I leave you can get her up and see if she'll eat anything. I'm heading into Belknap to wire for the ransom money and will wait for a reply. I'm sure Mr. Big Bucks will meet our demands. Boys, by the time that girlie gets home we'll be halfway to Mexico." Wayland grinned and realized he hadn't felt this good in a long time and was sober to boot, he thought. He needed a clear head to complete this job. He would have plenty of time to quench his thirst once they got south of the border.

As Wayland was getting into the truck, Jack went over and talked to him. Orton couldn't hear what they were talking about. A few minutes later Wayland got out of the truck and went to Orton.

"Orton," he said, "When you two get to the Breaks camp I want you to go up to the top of lookout mesa. If you see anyone coming yell to Jack and he and the girl will go out the back way. You can follow them. Got it!"

"Dad," Orton said, "I don't think anyone yet will...."

"Damn it Orton," Wayland yelled, "I don't care a crap what you think. You will do as you are told. Do you understand?"

Orton nodded yes.

"Good, Jack's the only one who knows the back way out of here and where we'd meet up should anything go wrong. Got it?" Wayland said.

Again, Orton, head low, nodded yes. As he began to look up, he was met by Wayland's hand that slapped him hard across the face. The stinging pain caught him by surprise. In anger, he stepped toward his dad.

Wayland quickly put his hand on his gun. "Don't make me do it boy. Now you two get the girl in the wagon and go and you make sure to get up on that rock."

Jack, holding the wagon's horse, watched the whole thing. He looked over to the cabin, grinned, and spat a wad of tobacco onto the dry earth. "It's going to be a beautiful morning," he said.

Before he left in the truck, Wayland went over to Jack. "Keep an eye on Orton," he said. "Be careful of that one, I don't trust him. Gotta go. I need to make Belknap by noon. You know what to do if I'm not back in two days?"

"Sure do, Pa," Jack said, "I'll take care of things here."

Wayland left. Orton and Jack led the girl out to the wagon and lay her down in the flat of the long bed. After loading the remainder of the supplies, they made their way to the Break's camp. They then led Sue Ann Yancy to the bedroom and tied her again to the bed posts.

She hadn't eaten anything but took several sips of water to quench her thirst. With her now dusty brown dress that had once been blue and her hair out of place, Orton hardly recognized her as the girl he had abducted the day before. What are we doing, he thought. What would Harshaw think?

Jack waved his hand high. "Get up on the mesa like dad said." Orton nodded.

Orton grabbed a canteen of water and a slab of jerky. He would be on that rock until near sundown. As Orton headed up the draw to the mesa trail, Jack turned and went into the bedroom.

The coolness of the morning was leaving the mesa as Orton sat down on a rock. Far down below he could view the top of the cabin. Jack was inside with Sue Ann Yancy. Orton felt helpless and once more alone. On one side of the table rock was a straight drop of over 100 feet. It would be so easy Orton thought, to take a few more steps and end it all. He would be through with the agony he was feeling that Miss Yancy was experiencing. He would be through with the hatred of his father and brother. His mother got out, why couldn't he. But he knew if he left, he was the only one who could possibly save the girl from his father's deadly intentions. Somehow, he had to find a way; he would find a way. If Carl Wayland could make plans maybe his son could, too.

Orton rarely looked about for anyone coming. He and Jack knew that no one would be looking this early and not here. Jack wanted to be with the girl. That was his plan. A few times Orton heard the door to the cabin open and shut. Jack would come out, feed and water the horses, or walk down to the river for water, then he'd wave to Orton and go back inside. When the sun was high overhead, he saw Jack lead Miss Yancy to the outhouse. Her blindfold was still on and she walked at a slow unsteady pace. Once she stumbled and Jack caught her. Orton noticed that Jack had his gun out and was talking quietly to his hostage. She stepped into the outhouse and came out a few minutes later. They both went back into the cabin.

Along toward sundown Orton climbed down off his watch post and went back to the cabin. Jack was sitting at the table with a bottle of his dad's whiskey. Orton never said a word and went to the back room. Miss Yancy looked about the same as she did this morning with her hands and feet tied to the bed posts.

"Did she eat anything?" Orton asked.

"No," Jack answered. "She hasn't eaten a damn thing since we got here. She did drink a few cups of water though."

"Has she said anything, asked for anyone?" Orton asked.

Jack laughed, "Yeah, after we came back from her crap break or her piss break or whatever she asked me to let her go. Said she'd give me her little diamond ring if I did. Pretty, isn't it?" Jack pulled the ring off the top of his small finger and showed it to Orton. Orton shook his head.

"Hey!" Jack said, "I didn't lie to her. I or we plan to let her go right? So, the ring is now mine."

As soon as Jack put the ring back on his finger his hand went back to the gun at his side.

I missed my chance, Orton thought. I won't let the next one go by.

But the chance never came. Jack spent the night in the girl's room with the door bolted from the inside.

From his perch atop the mesa shortly after noon on the next day, Orton could see Wayland riding back to the cabin. Wayland was riding fast and that meant that the hostage deal was probably on. Although the rider was a half mile away, he'd be at the camp in a few minutes. Orton decided to stay where he was. He would let his dad tell him when to come down, if at all.

Wayland pulled into the camp, got off his horse and ran inside the cabin. A few minutes later he came out and called to Orton. "C'mon down boy but make sure you take one good long look about before you do."

Halfway down the trail Orton had an idea.

# 8

# ORTON'S PLAN

AS HE CAME AROUND THE BACKSIDE OF THE CABIN ORTON was limping and grimacing in pain. Wayland and Jack were out front talking and when the old man saw Orton he yelled. "What the hell happened to you?"

"I, I, was coming down and slipped," Orton said. "I was trying to get down as fast as I could. You seemed to be in a hurry to tell me something." Orton's pants were ripped open at the knee and blood oozed through the material.

Wayland took off his hat and slapped Orton in the face with it. "Don't you dare lay your idiocy on me boy," he said, gritting his teeth in anger. He spit a wad of tobacco into the ground at Orton's feet. "Now you're about worthless, and I had plans for you. But you can't drive the truck in your condition. Damn it boy," Wayland yelled again.

Orton sat down in the sand and held his knee.

"Anything broke?" Wayland asked.

"I don't think so," Orton said. "It just hurts to walk."

Wayland turned to Jack. "You're going to have to drive the truck to Crow Springs. Do you think you can manage that?"

"Sure," Jack said. "What's going on?"

Wayland related how he set things up to get the money and exchange the girl. "I paid the telegraph operator five bucks to get lost for an hour or so. Then I telegraphed Great Falls and...."

Jack jumped in "You know how to run one of them telegraph machines?"

Wayland answered, "Yup, another little trade I learned in prison years ago. Some old guy taught me, said it would come in handy someday. This is the someday. Anyway, as I was saying, I let the police and the bank president, the girl's father, know that we had her and would release her unharmed once they delivered $50,000. I got a reply some twenty minutes later and they agreed but first they had to have proof that we were the ones who had the girl. She's wearing a diamond ring on one of her fingers and after we bring that to Crow Springs, they will get the money and drop it off. So, Jack you go in and get the ring off the girl's finger. Then take the horse to George's camp and drive the truck to the Springs. They will be waiting for you at the gas station there tomorrow morning. They won't harm you as long as we have the girl. You then arrange to pick up the money and get back here.   Once we have the dough, we'll telegraph them again and let them know where to pick up the girl. Do you think you can handle that?"

Jack nodded yes. "What if they folla me?" he asked.

"You let them know that if they do, we'll be watchin' from afar and the girl will die," Wayland replied.

Jack smiled and whistled, "Fifty thousand dollars; Damn, we can buy a nice ranch with that and have plenty left over for the senoritas."

Wayland smiled and put his arm around Jack. He then whispered into his ear. Jack smiled again and nodded. "Got it," he said, allowed, "I got it."

Jack went into the cabin and came out a few minutes later holding the ring in his hand.

"Here," Wayland said holding out an empty tobacco tin. "Put it in here so you don't lose it."

Jack put the ring in the can and then put it in the saddle bag of the horse. He then got on the horse and was about to ride down the trail when Wayland stopped him. "Make sure you tell 'em that if you're not back in three days they won't ever see Miss Sue Ann Yancy again."

Jack rode off heading to George's camp.

Looking down on his son, Wayland again shook his head, "I had you figured to go instead but you had to go lame on me. I should just shoot you like I do a lame horse. But we need you to keep that truck running. So, we're stuck with ya. Get up outa that dirt and get into the cabin."

Orton faked his struggle to get up and hobbled into the shack. He then lay down on the bed, a feigned expression of hurt on his face. "Sorry Paw," he said. "I didn't mean to I just…"

"Shudup," Wayland said. "I don't want to hear any more from your sorry ass. I'm tired and going into the back room and sleep for a while. Your brother won't be back until tomorrow night, so I'm stuck with you." He then went into the bedroom and bolted the door.

Orton had ripped his pants and scratched his knee with a sharp rock on purpose. He figured his dad would probably want him to go into town instead of Jack whose face would now be known to the law. By staying behind, he hoped to ensure no harm would come to Miss Yancy. But as he lay back on his bunk, he heard noise from the back room and a muffled groan from under a gag.

As the sun began to rise on that cool October morning, Carl Wayland stepped out of the cabin and walked toward the Missouri river. He'd had a pull of his whiskey for breakfast and was feeling good. I'm going to miss this old place, he said to himself, but soon I'll have another like it in Mexico only bigger with horses and cattle.

As he began to pee and suck in the fresh cool air, he hardly heard Orton come up behind him.

"What you doin?" he asked finishing his duty and turning to Orton.

"You're going to kill that girl aren't you dad?" Orton said.

"What's it to you anyway, it's my call not yours," Wayland said. He went to grab his gun, but it was back in the cabin. He looked at Orton. In his hand was a silver knife with a deer antler handle.

Holding the knife out in front of him Orton said, "I can't let you do that."

Wayland laughed. "You really think you can take me boy. Hell one, you don't know the first thing about fightin' and two you ain't got the guts to kill a man like I know how to kill a man. Put the knife away. We've got things to do."

"I'm not letting you near that girl again," Orton said breathing heavily, looking directly into the eyes of his father. Orton could feel the blood pulsing through the veins in his neck. In a flash he remembered all the moves with a knife Harshaw had taught him. He never thought he would have to use it.

For an instant fear flushed into Wayland, but then he let it pass. He saw a young man, who was trying to be a hero, a young man who probably wanted the girl for himself. There will be one less heading south and one less to split that money with, he thought.

"Tell ya' what, Orton. If you and Miss Yancy want to go off together after we get the money, I'll let you do that," Wayland said, and as he did, he bent over and pick up a piece of driftwood and slammed it at Orton.

Orton stepped back as the stick caught his arm. Wayland made a lunge for Orton, who stepped quickly aside. Orton slipped a leg under his dad's leg, and Carl went tumbling to the ground. In a blink, he was back on his feet and took a hard right swing at Orton. The young man stepped into his father and the knife found a place between the ribs. Wayland's eyes showed the horror of his last few seconds of life, the knife deeply embedded in his chest.

"Damn son, you are fast with that blade," Wayland smiled as he dropped to his knees into the sand. "Jack had said you were good with that thing....". Falling backward into the sand Wayland looked up forever and one last time at the blue Montana sky. His eyes stayed open.

Orton stood over him. "My God," he said aloud. "What did I do?"

It was not within Orton Wayland to take a life. Slowly his legs buckled out from underneath him, and he sat in the pebbly sand next to his dead father. A strange numbness overtook him. Then the brief moment of regret for what he had done past him by.

Wind rustled in the cottonwood trees around them. The Missouri river flowed on. An odd smile remained on his father's face. Perhaps, Orton thought, his dad had finally found that ranch in Mexico or maybe another place of peace away from the harshness of life. The only other time he'd seen his father smile was when the boy fell after being tripped from an unseen boot that sent a little boy flying to the living room floor or into the dirt. Carl Wayland smiled, too, when he came home drunk, taking pleasure in calling his wife names a young man could little understand but made the woman cry. A young man who saw his father's smile while holding his brother Jack and saying, "my good boy, my only good boy."

Jack, Orton thought, Jack is coming, Jack will be back soon. The girl is in the cabin tied to the bed. Orton stood up. "Time to lay you to rest old man."

With all his strength he picked up the body and took it down closer to the river. Slightly above the water plain the sandy earth was softer and without rocks.

Orton ran back to the cabin and got a shovel. At a furious pace he began to dig.

"Jack is coming back," he said to himself, and he dug faster.

When he had a trench four feet down two feet across and the length of a man, he walked over to the body that lay face up amidst the dead grasses and prairie sorrel.

Orton noticed the knife that was still stuck in his

father's chest. "I can't bury you like that," he said, grabbing the knife. As he pulled it out Orton's stomach convulsed. He wretched into the pit and threw the knife in with it. Then he rolled the corpse into the grave.

With an urgency knowing that his brother would take revenge for this deed, Orton refilled the pit. When the grave was smooth and level, he walked down the shoreline and pulled out sage and other brush replanting it atop the sand. He then collected dead grasses and river litter and spread it over the site. With a ball of tumble weed he brushed his foot tracks away back to the cabin. Taking off his boots he retraced his steps and scattered more grass and litter over the area.

Looking back from where he had come, he could not tell that two men had met here and only one returned.

"I'm the only person who will ever know," Orton thought as he looked down toward the river. He could not tell exactly where he'd dug the grave. Jack wouldn't either. As he turned to head back to the cabin, he whispered a quiet "goodbye."

Inside the cabin he untied Sue Ann Yancy. He ungagged her mouth but left the blindfold on. He quickly gathered his bed roll, clothes case, a canteen of water, an oil lantern, extra kerosene, and went to the buggy. He put the bedroll down and lay his case at one end. After hitching up the horse, he went back and gently took the girl out to the wagon. He lay her down on his bedroll, making sure her head rested on the case. He covered her with Wayland's bedroll. The mid-morning air was cool, but the rising sun told Orton to hurry.

Before leaving he took one last check of the place. He wanted it to look like he, his father and the girl had gone together. He knew that Jack would think they had all gone into Fort Belknap to the north. Orton, however, was heading southeast, away from Jack's direction.

Orton left a bottle of Wayland's whiskey on the table. That will slow him down, Orton thought, and Jack knows where the rest of the bottles are kept. Who knows, maybe that liquor will keep Jack here for a week or more waiting for Wayland's return. If Jack had the money and no one ever came back, what would he do then? Orton decided he didn't give a damn.

With a slap of the reins the wagon bolted out of the cabin area and down the trail to George's camp. The trail wound down and around, up, and down over the sandstone formations of the break. The rough ride at times caused Orton to pause and slow down knowing the girl in the back was getting the ride of her life.

"Jack is on his way, gotta keep moving," Orton thought. Only once did he stop and get in the back with the girl. He pulled the blanket back, and she lay there not moving but breathing with heavy sighs.

"Please Miss Yancy," he said, "trust me. I'm not going to hurt you. Here, please take a drink of this. You probably haven't had anything to drink or eat for a while."

Orton unscrewed the top of the canvas canteen and set it aside. He then put a hand under her head and lifted it upward while grabbing the canteen and putting it to her mouth. At first, she shook her head no. But when a little water hit her parched lips, she took a sip, then a long drink. When Orton pulled the jug aside, she grabbed it with both hands and drank again.

Good, Orton thought, she wants to survive. She is tougher than she looks.

"No one's going to harm you again," Orton assured her. "I'm taking you to safety, back to your father and friends. Now lay back and try to sleep. We have a long ride ahead of us." He took his hand out from under her head and lay it back on the case.

Almost noon, Jack's on his way. They passed George's camp and Orton did not slow down. Another mile and the land began to flatten out and the road became smoother. Three more miles and they came to an intersection in the road. Straight ahead would take them to Fort Belknap, left to Fort Benton and Great Falls, Orton went right. He now knew that he had little chance of meeting up with Jack. Orton began to feel more at ease.

The graveled road was dusty, so Orton did what many wagon drivers did: he put a neckerchief around his nose and mouth. A black Ford passed him heading west. Orton waved and the driver waved back. He knew that no one would be able to give a description of him should the law enforcement folks begin to ask questions. There would probably be a reward for information leading to the arrest of those who took the bank president's daughter.

Orton hoped to make it to Roy, a little town of several hundred people north of Livingston. He and Harshaw had once made a house call there to fix a farmer's broken tractor. He knew there was a telegraph office there too at the spur line railroad yard.

Sunset came six hours later. Roy was still ten miles away. Orton pushed on, seeing the road by the scant light of a half moon. He had stopped occasionally at streams to water the horse and attend to his passenger.

Hours later he pulled into the farmer's yard. Orton noticed that electric lines had not reach this place yet. Most of the buildings were dark except for the house lit by kerosene lanterns. He stopped the wagon by the front door. He went to the back of the buckboard, got on his knees, and crawled next to Miss Yancy.

"Listen", he said. "I hope you can hear me. You are safe now. I'm bringing you to people who will get you back to your father. They will give you food and water. I'm going to pick you up again now so please do not try to fight me or scream. Okay. You will be all right."

Orton got out of the wagon. By pulling on the heavy wool bedroll the girl lay on he was able to pull her toward him. He let her legs slide over the edge and when they did, he put one arm under them and the other under her shoulders. He then carried her to the door of the house. With his foot he kicked knocked the door.

"Who is it, who's there?" a voice called from inside the house.

"Help me," Orton said, "I need your help."

The door opened. The farmer stood with a rifle in his hand. A few feet behind him stood his wife.

"What, what happened?" the farmer asked. "Did you have an accident, what?"

Still wearing his mask and in a muffled voice Orton said, "I think this is the girl who was kidnapped out of Great Falls a few days ago. Her name is Sue Ann Yancy. I found her on the road."

"You mean that bank president's daughter?" the farmer asked. "I heard about her in town yesterday."

The farmer's wife spoke, "bring the girl in here and lay her on the couch. I'll get her some water."

Orton lay her down on the large couch and went back to the doorway. "I've got to get back to the cows," he said. "They need milkin'. Please take good care of her and make sure she gets back to her home."

Orton ran out and hopped onto the wagon.

"Wait," the farmer yelled. "Who the hell are you? Stop I say, wait."

Orton slapped the reins of the horse and sped off. He

heard the house door slam behind him. As he drove away tears began to flow from his eyes, down his cheeks followed by heaving shaking sobs. He was finally free of this tragedy. Finally free of his father's wrath and free for a moment of silent prayer that the girl he had saved would be back with her loved ones. A kind of love that Orton had never known.

# 9

# THE ROAD TO MALTA

HIS HEART HUNG HEAVY AS HE DROVE THE BUCKBOARD down the prairie road. The moon would be setting in a few hours and total darkness would come. When it did, he'd have to find a place to sleep for a few hours and then get north to Malta and the train station. In the distant hills, miles from where he was, a lone coyote howled at the same moon.

"I'm not much of a Godly man," Orton said aloud into the darkness, but I ask you God for forgiveness for what I did to my father. I hope you'll understand. Please help Miss Yancy and know that I meant her no harm."

The wagon plodded off into the night. The only sound was the clop of horse hooves on the road and the squeal of a wagon axle that needed grease. A constant Montana wind chilled Orton to the bone. He reached behind him and pulled the bed roll up around his shoulders and drove on. Try as he might, he still could not get the picture out of his mind of his father lying in the sand, face up staring into the sky. "Damn it," he said, "what the hell did I do?"

Hours later after crossing the Missouri river bridge and in near total darkness, Orton pulled off the road into a grove of cottonwoods. By the light of his oil lamp, he unhitched the horse from the wagon and tied her to a low hanging branch. Getting out the last bag of oats, he dumped it into a bucket.

"Not sure what I am going to do with you when I get to Malta," Orton said to the horse as it munched its way through the grain. "But I'll figure something out."

When the sun went down, the temperature went with it. Orton clapped his hands together and he had to stomp his feet to get them warm. The warmth came grudgingly so he climbed onto the wagon and covered himself with the wool blankets and felt. He wasn't sure of the time; he only knew he was looking forward to sunup and warmer weather.

But the morning sun didn't wake him. Instead, he was pelted with an icy hard rain. It was daylight. He was unsure how many hours he'd slept but he felt refreshed. The day was dark, windy, and wet. Tossing the bedroll aside, he grabbed a can of beans under the buckboard and opened them with the axe. The beans were almost frozen in the can but with a stick he managed to scoop them into his mouth. He wanted to eat the last can but decided to ration it being unsure of when his next meal might come. He re-hitched the horse and took again to the road.

It was wide open prairie all the way to Malta and nothing to stop the wind that tortured him with the cold rain. He pulled his hat down almost over his eyes and wrapped his neck scarf over the hat and his ears. His hands were so cold he could barely hang onto the reins.

A hundred more miles to go. Wishing the cold rain and wind to stop would not make it so. Orton again pulled the felted sleeping pad over his head and around his shoulders. He held this makeshift tent with one hand while the other held the leather straps guiding the horse.

A car honked behind him. Orton steered the wagon off to the right so the car could pass. As he did a shiny black Ford pulled alongside. A window came down. A youth, about his age, stuck out a fist and shook it.

"Damned Indian," the youth yelled. "Get the hell off the road."

Laughter erupted inside the car. From a quick glance, Orton saw a bottle pass to the driver and tipped upwards. The car window closed, and the car sped into the greyness. Orton noticed a weaving from side to side as he followed it out of sight. Yesterday's traveler plodded on.

At the bottom of a coulee was a small pond of settled

rainwater. Around it was the last green clumps of autumn sweet grass. Orton stopped and let the horse drink its fill. He grabbed a cup and drank the liquid, doing little to quench a gnawing hunger. The rain had eased a bit and the wind was not as bad in this hallow. He shivered in the damp cold and again stamped his feet. His clothes felt wet to the skin. He couldn't stop the shivering.

Then he remembered the oil lantern. He had tossed in an extra can of lamp oil. He figured he only needed it for one more night, so he lit the lantern and turned up the wick. His hands felt the heat as it rose out of the glass chimney. He put his face over the light and let the oily warmth wash over him, enjoying the sweet smell of the burnt liquid. After a few minutes the shivering stopped.

With the lantern between his legs and the wool felt around him, Orton soon dried his jacket and shirt. He also noticed his mind was a little clearer. "Cold and damp can do strange things to man," Harshaw had once told him, "The danger sign comes with the intense shivering. Get warm or die like many a cowboy who couldn't out on the open plains."

Harshaw's memory brought a smile to Orton. Someday, he thought, he'd get back to Lewiston after he'd made his fortune in Detroit, and he would thank Harshaw proper.

The road stretched for endless miles broken only by the occasional coulee and sage covered valley. As he traveled his mind kept going back to all that happened. Orton Wayland was a good-hearted young man kicked into a damned if you do damned if you don't situation. At times his mind played the "what if" game. What if he could have gotten the girl away from his father and Jack without the killing? What if he would have only knocked his father out, tied him up, and then taken the girl to safety? Yes, that's what he should have done. Yet, he knew that Carl would have caught up to them and would have killed them both. He cursed his luck. He searched his soul for answers, but none came. Fact one, he had killed his father. There was no escaping that. Fact two, Jack would be looking for him. He thought of his mother and wondered where she might be. He wondered if he would ever see her again. What would she think of this whole ugly mess he had gotten himself into?

Orton screamed into the empty grasslands: "Why didn't you take me with you, why did you have to leave me behind?" He hung his head and sobbed. The horse turned its' head back toward Orton and then back toward the road and plodded on. For a moment Orton envied the horse whose only lot in life was to pull a wagon. Alone in this world, the horse could survive on grass and water. It could wander freely if let go to find food and shelter. No worries, no cares.

"Right now, horse, I'd trade places with you." Wherever he looked he saw the face of his father, the face of Jack and of Miss Sue Ann Yancy. While he felt cold and alone, he was somehow glad the girl was now safe. He saw her back with her father and friends. And that thought jolted him back into a new reality. Her father would not take this kidnapping lightly. He would use his money and resources to find out who took his little girl away from him. Police from all over Montana would soon be on the trail of three men who had ravaged his daughter. Had they caught Jack? Did the farmer give a description to the police of the horse, wagon and masked rider who had delivered Sue Ann to safety?

The farmer would not have had a telephone, so he couldn't notify the police until today. Montana is a big place, and he had put many miles behind him since he left the farm. If the police caught up with him, would he tell them that he killed his father? Would the fact that he did it to save the girl's life keep him from the gallows? How many years would he spend in prison?

I can't think about that, Orton said to himself. I've got to make it to Malta and get on a train for Detroit. Concentrate on what you have got to do. Do not act like any kind of desperado; that will only give you away. Keep your hat on so no one can see your blond hair. Sue Ann Yancy would give the police a description of him, Jack, and his father. She would tell them we were on our way to Mexico. They would concentrate checking the roads and rail stations to the south and west of Roy and the Missouri breaks area. With that thought Orton breathed a momentary sigh of relief. Then the picture of his father lying in the sands of the Missouri river would come back to haunt him once again.

A truck with cattle passed him. The driver waved and Orton waved back.

"Oh, with a truck like that," he said to the horse," I could be in Malta in a few hours." Ten hours of wagon travel would get him halfway there. "We will see it tomorrow evening, old paint, and then we'll part ways."

He planned on selling the horse and buggy and getting a train ticket to Detroit. He hoped that the city was not windy like Montana. He remembered hearing that Chicago was a windy city but knew nothing about the motor city.

"I can't put up with this constant wind anymore," he said aloud. And as he did so, a full gust hit him dead on and nearly tore his hat from his head and the wool felt from his hand.

That night in a coulee halfway to Malta, he ate the last can of beans. Orton slept soundly in the back of the wagon. He had his bed roll and the one he had gotten for the girl. Using both, one on top and one below, he found comfort from the raw elements of the plains.

Sometime in the middle of the night he looked down toward the end of the wagon. There stood his father, the knife still stuck in his chest. A red flame flickered up and down his body.

"I've come back for you boy. Here I am, look at what you did," Wayland pointed to the knife. "This is your blade and I've come to give it back." With that the figure pulled the knife from his chest and held it menacingly toward Orton.

Orton sat upright and screamed, "No!" His heart raced fast, sweat trickling down the back of his neck... A dream, Orton thought, only a bad dream. He's gone. Orton lay down again in a restless slumber.

By morning's light without a sun, Orton pulled out of the coulee. The horse had grazed and watered enough to make this last push to Malta. On the flat prairie the wind found him once more. The rain had stopped and, with the lantern going, he was warm and dry. He could see his breath and knew that it could snow. Something he was not prepared for.

He heard a rattling noise from the bed of the wagon. He looked behind and saw the last can of beans now empty. Beans, Orton thought. When I make my money in Detroit, I'm never going to eat another bean in my life. I'll be living on beef, baked potatoes, and onions. He could almost taste it, but the thought did little to quench his gnawing hunger.

Down into a valley and around a corner Orton came upon a cowboy on a quarter horse. He pulled to a stop.

"Hi ya'," the rider said. "Where ya' headed?"

"Down the road a piece," Orton answered, "dropping off this wagon for a friend. You seem to be a long way from nowhere."

The cowboy grinned and said:" Waiting for my boss to decide what to do with that." He pointed to the bottom of the hill.

There, in a mangled mess amidst rocks and big boulders, lay a once shiny black car on its side. Smoke was rising from the engine.

"Two boys, looked to be pretty liquored up and on a wild side ride missed that turn you just came around." The cowboy shook his head. "One guy we found in the car; the other was underneath it. The slab wagon took 'em away an hour ago. What a waste. Nice car, too."

To Orton the car looked familiar but with all the damage he couldn't be certain.

"Yeah, too bad. Well good luck with it," Orton nodded and slapped the reins hard. The animal bolted into a fast trot.

It was getting dark when he pulled into the little town of Malta. This was but a train stop for cattle and grain loading. The main street had several saloons and a diner. Orton dug into his pocket and found 38 cents, all of which he'd discovered under the seat of the buckboard.

The town on a Thursday night was quiet. A few cars were in front of the diner and more by the saloons. Orton drove the wagon around back and found a hitching post and tied up the horse. He entered a side door, took a seat at the counter, and grabbed a menu.

A gum chewing waitress in her late-40s, wearing a nurse type hat, walked up. "What'll ya' have cowboy?"

Scanning his options, Orton found what he was looking for. "I'll have the burger plate with fries and onions, "he said. "Does that come with a drink?"

The waitress looked down on him, chewed her gum twice and said, "No."

"Then I'll just have water," he said. Another three more cents and he could have gotten a glass of milk or coffee. He'd leave a three-cent tip for the gum chewer.

"You must have been hungry, most people don't eat all of Al's greasy fries," the waitress said as Orton paid his bill.

Orton smiled. It had been a while since he'd had a full meal and he felt good.

"Excuse me but can you tell me if there is a blacksmith in this town?" Orton asked, "I've got a horse and buggy I'd like to sell."

The waitress thought a minute and then walked over to the cook's take out. "Al" she said, "does Bar H still deal with buggies and horses?"

A thin face that had not seen a razor in a while appeared, a roll-your-own cigarette hanging from his lips. "Yeah, I think so. Why?"

"This guy out here wants to sell his horse and buggy," she answered.

"Have 'em talk to Joe Steel out there, that's where I would start anyway," the cook said.

"Thank you," Orton called out. The cook waved and nodded. After getting directions to the Bar H, Orton went back to the wagon. Just as he was untying the horse, he heard a voice in the darkness.

It was the waitress. "You don't have a place to stay for the night do you, son?"

"No ma'am I don't," Orton said.

"What're you going to do?" she asked.

"Well, I thought I'd go back out abouts where I'd come and find a place off the road like I had been doing for a while now," Orton explained. "I've got a good bedroll and will sleep in the buckboard; it's not too bad."

"It's too dangerous on the road at night," she said. "I can't let you do that, especially in this damn wind. Tell you what, I've got a place four blocks down here on Main. It's an upstairs apartment. You can use the sofa. But only for one night, you understand?"

Orton couldn't believe his luck. "Yes ma'am, I do, only for tonight, I leave in the morning," he said.

"By the way I can't pay you anything."

"No need," she said. "I've got a son a little older than you. He's down in Arizona now with the rodeo circuit. I hope to God someone's watching out for him."

The cook appeared in the back door. "Judy, get in here, you've got a customer."

She quickly gave Orton directions to the house and the place behind her building to put the horse and buggy.

After stashing the buckboard and horse into an empty garage, Orton found his way into the waitresses' apartment. It was small with a kitchen, living room, bedroom, and, Orton noticed, a room with indoor plumbing. Rodeo trophies of bucking broncs and brass horseshoes adorned the table. Orton sat down on the sofa. He thought he'd wait until the waitress came home in an hour or two.

Sunlight filtered through cotton curtains opened his eyes. He looked about. At the table sat the waitress with coffee in one hand and a cigarette in the other. He pulled aside a thin blanket. He noticed someone had taken off his boots.

"Honey," the waitress said," I've seen some tired guys come and go but you take the prize. It was all I could do to put you down on that couch. Good thing your boots were off. By the way you talk in your sleep."

"Huh, what, what did I say?" Orton asked his heart beginning to race.

"Something about a girl being safe. You mumbled a bit. I couldn't quite get all of it," the waitress said.

"Don't know what that was all about," Orton said nervously. 'What time is it? I should be on my way."

"Hold on, Bar H won't open until nine, so you've got an hour to have my special eggs ala Canadian bacon," she said. "I've learned a few things from Al. Anyway, I'm celebrating."

Smiling, she held up a ten-inch-high stature of a cowboy on a bucking bronc. "This came in the mail this morning along with a check for $20 dollars. Timmy took a first place in Pueblo. So, get your sore butt up to this table and eat."

Seeing her face swell with pride warmed Orton's heart. He thought this is how it could have been with his own mother. He wondered for a moment where she might be, who she might be with. He said a silent prayer that she was safe.

"Congratulations," he said, "I hope the best for him."

# 10

# TICKET TO NOWHERE

JOE STEEL AT THE BAR H WAS ADAMANT. "SON, I CAN'T GIVE you a penny more than $19 dollars for that horse, wagon, lantern, and everything else you've tossed in. Hell, I had to feed that sorry horse a full bag of oats when you brought him in here. Felt sorry for him. Now you can take the money or leave."

Orton had hoped to get $20 but 19 would do. "I'll take it, Mr. Steel; you drive a hard bargain."

When he collected his money, he returned to the horse. "Good by old horse; we've put on a few miles you and I." With that he ruffled the horses' mane with his hand and then began the long walk to the train station.

"How much for a ticket to Chicago?" Orton asked the ticket man behind the counter.

"Chicago, Chicago, let's see here," the ticket man

looked at his charts. "That'll be $36 dollars second class."

"36 dollars?" Orton look at the man behind a pair of thick glasses in disbelief. "All I've got is 19."

"Sorry son I can't help ya," he shot back. "21 dollars will get you to St. Paul. You might find work there for enough money to get you to Chicago."

"I still need two more dollars," Orton said shaking his head.

"Hey, right now there is a gent looking for a few guys to help load lumber from his trucks onto rail cars. Tell you what, I'll hold a ticket for you and if you can get work come back and get it. Names Jensen and he is down in the yard a ways. Train won't leave until three tomorrow, so you have time." With that he put Orton's ticket under a rock on the counter.

Orton stepped back from the ticket window, looked down into the yard and spotted four trucks loaded high with lumber. Well, he thought to himself, looks like I'm working my way across country. He picked up his bed roll and blankets and headed for the yard.

"Name's Joe Willard," Orton said offering a hand to a big man in a bowler hat in the first truck in line. On the side of the truck was the name "Jensen Sawmill and Logging." "Heard you were looking for some loaders."

A man with tree trunk shoulders got out of the truck and shook Orton's hand. "That I am young man, that I am. Pay is $2 a day and I'm glad you came along. I've got two other guys I found hanging around the Stockman's, but you look in better shape than those two. My drivers will help too. After I unload, I'll go back tonight and get another and be back tomorrow morning. If you can be here at six, you can earn another two dollars. We should be done by one or two. Train don't leave til' three. I'm Ada Jensen by the way."

"Two day's work, you bet, I'll be here," Orton said and with quick addition he figured he'd have more than enough money for his ticket and a few trips to the dining car. "When do we start?"

Jensen looked down the rail line. "About 20 minutes. They are getting the cars ready now. You have any gloves? This is all rough-cut wood, and it can be hard on the hands even as rough as yours are."

"No, no, I don't," Orton said.

"That's okay kid," Jensen said. "I've got some extras you can use just give 'em back tomorrow when we get done."

Orton nodded a thanks when Jensen gave him a pair of thick rawhide gloves.

When the rail cars were lined up, the unloading, loading began. The steady cold north wind felt good as Orton sweated and strained under the long heavy pieces of cottonwood. He preferred this work more than driving an open wagon. He was glad to use his arms and hands again, and he thought about how in a few weeks he might be using them on an assembly line making cars in Detroit.

The crew worked until one o'clock, and Jensen called a lunch break. Orton smiled as he grabbed a bag of egg and bacon sandwiches that Judy, the waitress, had insisted he take with him for the trip. The drivers had their own home-made lunches, while the other two hires did a quick hike to the Stockman's, now open for lunch and beer.

By 2 pm they were back at it. Each piece of wood plank carefully lifted off the trucks and placed on the rail cars. Jensen was right. The trucks were emptied by 6:30 and Orton was handed his two dollars. Taking a cigar from his mouth, Jensen said, "You worked hard kid, that's more than I can say for those two other fellas. Hope to see you in the morning." With that he got back into his truck and was on his way to his mill for the last load.

The ticket office was closed for the day, but Orton figured he could pick up his ticket after work the next day. He took out his small wad of cash and added his new bills.

"What're you going to do with all that money?" Orton looked behind him. It was the other hire, the one name Mike.

"Oh," Orton said, "saving money for a car is all."

Mike's buddy Arnie came out from behind the cars zipping up his pants.

"How'd you like to make an extra dollar before the night's out?" Mike asked.

"What, how?" Orton asked.

"You see that green rail car down there with the blue door?" Mike said pointing down the line. "Inside is a guy who needs electrical equipment moved and restacked. He offered the job to Arnie and me, but we're a little busy tonight with a couple of women."

Orton thought about it for a minute and said "Sure, I could use an extra buck."

C'mon we'll take you down there," and Mike led the way with Arnie trailing behind.

When they got to the rail car Mike hopped up on an iron step, unbolted the door and shoved it open enough for entry. Mike stepped in and looked down. "C'mon on up."

Wait a second, Orton thought. Why did he have to open the car if the guy who needed help was supposed to be inside. "Maybe I'll pass on this job," he said and began to back away. As he did, he felt a gun in his ribs.

"Get up in the car kid, now!" Arnie demanded.

Orton did as he was told. When the three of them were inside Mike closed the door. The last sun of the day filtered through an open hatch in the roof. Orton knew he was in trouble.

"What do you want?" Orton asked. "I can give you a few dollars, just let me go."

Mike laughed. "Dumb kid, you know what we want, and we want all of it. Hand over the wad of bills you have there in your front pocket."

"Please, I beg you don't." Those were the last words of despair as Orton's lights went out and he fell to the floor. Arnie put the gun back into his shoulder holster.

"Geeze did you have to bang 'em so hard, he might be dead," Mike said.

"Like I give a bull's crap," Arnie said as he rolled Orton's body over and took the money from his pocket.

"We can't leave him lying here like this. If the railroad men find 'em, they'll ask questions and then what. We've got to stash him someplace."

As they pulled Orton's body to the back of the car Arnie bumped into something.

"What is it?" Mike asked.

"It's a big wooden boat," Arnie replied. "We can toss him in there and nobody will find 'em. I figure he'll be out for a while anyway."

"But what if he does come to?" Mike asked.

"Yeah, you're right Mikey. Help me find some rope and a rag and we'll truss him up and then put 'em in this damn boat," Arnie said.

When Orton was bound and gagged, the two men lifted and rolled him to the bottom of the boat.

Mike laughed. "Looks like the kid's going on a fishing trip. Where's he headed anyway?"

Arnie looked at the shipping tag on the front of the boat. "Hard to make out in this dim light. Looks like a place called, Hay, Hay, Hayward, Wisconsin. Where the hell is that?"

Mike shook his head. "I dunno, never heard of it."

As they closed and bolted the door to the rail car, Arnie said, "Good luck fishing kid. Hope you catch a big one." The two men laughed.

"You're too much, Arnie. Let's head down to the Stockman's. All this hard work has given me the thirst." Mike rubbed his hands together. "It's getting cold. Hey, why didn't we grab the kid's gloves?"

The next morning Ada Jensen had to scour the town to find three men to help unload his trucks. The ticket man waited until 3 o'clock and as the train pulled out heading East, he tore up Orton's ticket. Maybe the kid had other plans, he thought. Maybe he found a lady friend to share that money with and he couldn't bear to leave.

As he tossed the pieces of ticket into the open trash can a fierce north wind blew scattering stubs onto the floor.

"Shut that window," the station manager yelled at the ticket man. "We've got weather moving in from Canada. It'll be snowing by dinner time."

Leaving Malta, the Union Pacific made the last of its way across Montana and into North Dakota. After a dozen stops to drop off and pick up passengers and cargo, it made its way into Minnesota. By morning's light, six inches of heavy wet snow greeted the train as it entered St. Paul where the green rail car with the blue door was unhitched and hooked to a train bound for Wisconsin.

When the Chicago-Northwestern train reached the newly emerging tourist town of Hayward, a city surrounded by thick forests and hundreds of lakes, it stopped, and the green car's door was opened.

"Manifest says there's a boat in here for some guy named Townsend on the Chippewa Flowage," the transit manager said to his assistant as they boarded the car. "Darn thing was made in Seattle; they call it a Musky Fishing boat. Must be toward the back. There it is. We'll have to drag it to the doors and get Hank and Lyle to help us get it down." As the two men approached the boat, they heard a groaning noise, a muffled call for help.

"Johnny, did you hear that?" the transit man whispered. "Sounds like it came from around that boat. Better get your night stick ready." The two men had had to deal with train stowaways in the past. They walked up slowly to the where the boat sat.

The transit manager looked into the bottom of the boat. Orton's eyes were open, and he nodded his head. The manager removed the gag from Orton's mouth. "Help me," he said as his eye lids closed, and he again drifted into darkness.

"Looks like a young man in here and he's been bound and gagged." The manager felt for a pulse; it was slow but still there. Orton's skin was grey and cold.

"Johnny, go get Hank and Lyle. We got a kid in here in a bad way. Better call the sheriff and a doctor, too. Kid's near half froze to death," the manager said.

Four men gently pulled Orton from the boat, lifted him off the train car and took him into the station. They lay him on a bench. A small crowd gathered.

The sheriff soon arrived with a doctor in tow. Orton's breathing was shallow, his heartbeat irregular. The doctor tried to wake him. "Kid, Kid," he said, "can you hear me?" He tapped Orton's shoulder but there was no response. He took the kid's gloves off his hands and said aloud, "I wonder why he was wearing these? Probably saved his fingers."

The sheriff looked at the transit man. "Any idea where this kid came from or how he got on the train?" he asked.

"Could 'a been any number of stops from here to Seattle," the transit man said.

"We'll doc, as soon as he wakes up you get a hold of me," the sheriff said.

The doctor's name was Sutter. "We've got to warm this man up slowly," he said. "The kids in the late stage of hypothermia, and there is a bad gash on the back of his head." He looked up at the sheriff. "Without a wallet or money, it looks like he was robbed and dumped into that boat."

The sheriff sent his deputies to check the train cars for tramps and other illegal riders. He then asked the crowed of people standing around if anybody recognize the boy.

A few passengers walked up and looked at Orton and shook their heads no. The sheriff looked over the group a few minutes and then went to inspect the boat.

The station manager told the doctor that an ambulance was on the way to take the kid to the hospital.

"No, we can't afford to take him there in his condition with this flu epidemic hitting the town. The best place would be my house," he said. "I've got a special room for such cases as this. My daughter is in training to be a nurse, too. Looks like she's got her first patient.".

With the deputy, Hank and Lyle from the train station, Doc Sutter brought Orton into the back bedroom of his home. Sutter opened a window and shut the door.

"What are you doing, doc?" the deputy asked. "I thought you needed to warm this kid up."

"I do and I will," Sutter explained, adding that the warming had to be done slowly or heat shock would kill him quick.

"Last winter they brought a logger into the hospital almost froze stiff like this lad, only he was awake and telling us not to fuss with him. He appeared drunk but wasn't. We put him in a bed next to the stove and an hour later he was dead."

"Yeah, I remember that guy," the deputy said. "It was

Hoot Johnsen. We figured the cold killed him."

"It was that and the warm room both that did the guy in," Sutter said. "C'mon boys, give me a hand taking these old clothes off him. Hank, take off his boots."

Hank pulled Orton's boot, but it wouldn't budge. "Lyle," he said, grab that leg and hold it for me." Again, he pulled the boot, but it stayed in place.

Sutter and the deputy were taking off Orton's shirt. "What's the matter down there?" he asked.

"Doc," Hank said, "I think his feet are frozen in."

Sutter grabbed a boot, then felt the skin under the pant leg. "Peggy," he yelled out. "Peggy, are you in the front room?"

A voice from down the hall answered. "No, I'm working in your office, why?"

"Get me a number 2 surgical scissor quick," he said.

A moment later Sutter's daughter Peggy entered the room with a large pair of scissors.

"What happened daddy?" she asked, surveying the scene.

"I'll explain later. Right now we've got to get these boots off or we'll lose both these young man's feet to gangrene," he said.

Sutter cut through the leather of the cowboy boot. When it was loose enough, he pulled the boot off. He quickly did same on the other foot. Both feet were swollen to twice their size. When he pulled off the socks, Sutter shook his head. "I was afraid of this," he said. "Peggy, with your warm hands start slowly massaging that left foot, keep your hands working around the toes. I'll work on this foot."

Looking up at the other men in the room Sutter said, "Looks like we will be here awhile boys, so you fellas can go. Thanks for your help."

With a nod and wave the men left. Doc Sutter and his daughter Peggy spent the next three hours trying to warm and work circulation back into Orton's feet. At midnight Sutter stopped.

"Peggy," he said, "I'm going to need your help. I've got to amputate part of this boy's foot. There's no more I can do." He looked down at the foot Peggy had been warming. "You did a nice job honey. I am sure we can save that one. Get the chloroform and a mask for his face. We can't afford to have him wake up during this operation. Do you think you can handle that?"

Peggy's eyes widened. A touch of fear entered her soul.

"Yes," she said. "I can do it, Daddy."

"I know you can," he said gently. "Do a slow drip and watch his breathing. Now help me roll him. I need to get another rectal temp."

With her help, they rolled Orton onto his side. Doc Sutter inserted a rectal thermometer and waited a few minutes.

"Ninety one degrees," he said. "Good. He's come up ten degrees since we brought him in here. I think he is out of the danger zone now so we can amputate. Get that drip ready."

As his daughter got the anesthetic, Sutter prepared his scalpels, knives, and adjusted an overhead light at the end of the bed. Although tired from a long day of work, he knew this last job couldn't wait. Gangrene that must have set in early was now progressing faster as Orton's body warmed.

"Now," he said to Peggy, and she began a slow drip of the knockout fluid that would keep Orton asleep. Sutter then removed the three small toes on the right foot and went up an inch into the foot itself. Satisfied that he got it all, he sewed up the larger arteries, veins, and the skin flap. With Peggy's help, they wrapped the foot tight with gauzy bandages.

"Again, you did well darling," Sutter said looking at his daughter with pride. "I think we saved this boy's life. Now time we both got some sleep. He'll be okay for a while."

Orton Wayland lay on a high bank overlooking the Missouri River. His hands were tied behind his back, his feet bound at the ankles. He tried desperately to move but his body refused his command. Then he realized that if he did move, the earth would crumble beneath him, and he would roll into the current of the river. A river that ate away the sands below him. The river that had for centuries carved its way through sand and rock exposing sediments put down by rain, wind, snow, and heat. The Missouri river basin is part desert and part rain forest. Today it was a desert and, although the water was twenty feet away, he could taste it as if it were inches from his face. He could smell the moisture and feel the pulse of the surging waters. The sun, high overhead, beat down on him. Odd, he thought, he should be baking in this heat and yet he was cool almost cold. The grasses and mesquite on the opposite bank were brown and wilted in the hot air. The flat river plan stretched endlessly for miles. Am I dead, he thought. Is this hell? Will I lay here for eternity? Is this the judgement from God for what I did to my father? Time seemed to pass but the sun did not move. Orton lay there, his breathing rising and falling with the rhythm of the flowing water. It soon lulled him to sleep and when he awoke it was in darkness. His feet and hands were still tied. His head lay in the sand but behind his neck was a stabbing pain. His right foot ached. What happened as I slept, he thought. He tried to move his head to ease the throbbing and, when he did, he heard a voice.

"Well, you finally woke up after all these years." It was Jack, his brother. "I've been looking for you and here you are laying right next to our dear sweet dad."

"What," Orton said. "Where is he."

"Why, you are laying on top of him," Jack said, "and soon the current of this river will expose him to the world. By the way of I have a friend of ours here to say Hi."

From behind Orton came a woman's voice. It was Sue Ann Yancy.

"Help me, Orton, oh God, please help me," she said.

In an angered fury, Orton fought the ropes around his hands and feet and, as he did, the earth gave way beneath him. He rolled over and over and to finally lay face up in the water. Sinking into the depths, he looked up to see Jack laughing at him holding a girl in tears. Behind them were Mike and Arnie, laughing and waving goodbye.

Again, he struggled, and this time broke the ropes free. He sat up on a bed. A light came on overhead. Squinting into the whiteness he saw whom he thought was Sue Ann Yancy.

"You, you found me, how?" he asked. He looked around the room. "Sue Ann Yancy, where are we?"

# 11

# PEGGY

Peggy Sutter stood by the door. Her hand still on the light switch, her eyes wide with fright. "Dad," she yelled, "Dad, he's awake. Please lay back down on that bed. You are in a doctor's office. My father will explain to you what happened. Please lie back down." Her voice was quiet yet controlled.

The two looked at each other. A moment later Doc Sutter pushed by his daughter and went to Orton's bedside. Orton's gaze was on Peggy.

"Young man, look at me," Sutter said. "You have been through a tremendous ordeal." He took his hand and gently touched Orton's face and turned it toward his, looking directly into his eyes.

"My name is Ronald Sutter. I am a doctor, and you are in a bedroom at my home office. You were taken off a train three days ago suffering from hypothermia and a bad gash on the back of your head. This is my daughter Peggy; she has been attending to you these past days. We've had to be careful because of the flu epidemic in the city."

"What city?" Orton asked.

"Hayward," the doctor replied.

"Hayward, Hayward what?" said Orton.

"Hayward, Wisconsin," Sutter said. "It's a little town in the northern part of the state. You were found bound and gagged inside a boat that was on one of the train cars. First off, can you tell me what your name is and is there any family we can notify that you are alright. I am sure someone must be worried about you."

"My name is Orton...." Before he could say his last name, he thought about the kidnapping and if the law would be looking for him. He decided on a story. "I'm Orton, that's my last name I think, and how I got here I cannot remember." Orton looked away from the doctor and out the window. He sat pretending to remember his past when all the while he saw it flash quickly before his eyes. As he did, a truck sped by with "Jim's Electric" on a side panel. "I think my first name is Jim," he said and turned his focus back to the doctor. "Other than that, I can't recall anything."

"How many fingers do I have up?" the doctor asked.

"Two," Orton answered.

"Do you know who the president of the United States is?"

"No"

"Do you know what month or year this is?"

"No"

"Do you know how old you are?"

Orton though a moment. "No".

"How much is five plus five?"

Again, Orton looked off into the room and returned to look at the doctor. "Ten, I think."

"Look up at the light. I am going to hold a finger in front of your eyes, and I want you to follow it without turning your head." Sutter said.

Orton looked up at the light and followed Sutter's fingered commands. With a small rubber mallet, the doctor then did reflex tests on Orton's knee and arms. He then checked the wound on the back of Orton's head. "This seems to be healing nicely. Do you have any pain in your feet?"

Orton had noticed a throbbing pain in his right foot since the moment the light came on. "My right foot feels sore as hell. Whoops! I am sorry ma'am," he said, looking to Peggy who was now at her father's side.

"It's okay, Mr. Orton," she said, "I've heard much worse than that."

Sutter with a fake surprised look turned to his daughter. "What? Where have you heard worse language?"

Then he laughed. "I suppose in a town with loggers and fisherman you are bound to hear it all."

He then grabbed Orton's wrist and started counting his pulse. "Peggy, what we have here is a clear case of trauma induced amnesia. Whether he comes out of it I don't know. Usually, it doesn't last long. Some things he'll remember plain, and other things may never come back to him."

"Doctor Sutter, sir, I have no way to pay you for these services. But if you let me have my clothes and point me in the direction of the train or someplace else, I will find a job and I'll work to repay what I owe," Orton said.

Doc Sutter and his daughter turned to Orton. Orton looked into Peggy's eyes.

"What?"

Sutter put Orton's hand down and looked at him. "Jim, when you came in here both your feet were frost bitten. We had to cut your boots off to get at your swollen feet. We saved your left foot, but we had to amputate part of your right to save you from gangrene. I am sorry, son. You are going to have to learn how to walk all over again on that foot once it heals in three to four weeks. In the meantime, you are going to be my and Peggy's guest. How you pay your bill we can discuss later."

Orton lay back on the bed in stunned silence. An anger hovering between hate, disgust and pity began to rise inside of him. Two bums in Malta, Montana had done this to him, and he couldn't say a word because of his criminal involvement in taking a young girl hostage. He could still get to Detroit somehow, but would anyone hire him on an assembly line with half a foot? Was this a kind of purgatory or hell for what he had done to his father? Stuck now in Hayward, Wisconsin, and where in God's name is Hayward, Wisconsin? Maybe this is nothing more than a dream, he thought. Yes, I'll wake up on the train headed for Detroit and all will be well.

Doc Sutter gently tapped Orton on the shoulder. "Is there anything we can do for you now son?"

In a fit of rage Orton yelled out, "You are telling me part of my right foot is gone, gone.... like I am now some kind of a cripple? Is that what you are telling me? Tell you what, why don't you get my boots and my clothes, leave me the address for this place and I'll get out of your life, so I can restart mine, and I will pay you back for this office visit."

At those last words he put his head on his chest and began to cry. Self-pity had taken over. "Please," he said with tears in his eyes, "leave me alone. I know you did what you had to do. It's not your fault I'm here. I do not know what I am going to do. Leave me alone, please."

"Let's go, Peggy," Sutter said to his daughter. "Let's give Mr. Orton some time for himself."

Orton again put his head down and began to quietly sob.

The young nurse, who had been caring for this patient for the past three days, followed her father out the door. But before it closed all the way, she reopened it. With a display of her own anger and with tears in her eyes she said, "Mr. Orton, I'll be damned if I am going to let you give up on yourself. I have been taking care of you, massaging your feet and legs, changing your soiled clothes and bedpans. You are a strong healthy young man whose been through an ordeal, I grant you that, but I have seen many a man and woman in worst shape than you, and all have survived. And I'll tell you one thing:Dad and I are not going to give up on you. You are not going anywhere until my father says you are ready to go. Do you understand?"

Shaken from his forlorn stupor, Orton look up in stark surprise. "What?"

"You heard what I said, and tomorrow we are going to start on a program to get you back on your feet, well, what you have left of them anyway."

Doc Sutter had heard the whole thing and came back into the room. "Peggy," he said, "the patient asked to be alone. I think that we...."

"Hold on, Doc," Orton said. "My nurse is right. Miss Sutter, can you come here please?"

Peggy walked up to Orton's bedside. Orton looked into her eyes. "Thank you for all that you and your father have done for me," he said and smiled. "As long as I'm in your care, I'll do as you say. You're the boss. Okay?" He held out his hand for her to shake and she took it.

His eyes had been closed for three days and now Peggy looked into them for the first time. Under a shock of dusty blond hair were some of the bluest eyes she had ever seen in a man. Her hand was still in his and it felt invitingly warm, strong. She blushed and pulled her hand a way.

"Ah, ah, okay, yes, we will start tomorrow. Is tomorrow good with you Mr. Orton? No, we will, will start tomorrow," she said as she backed out of the room. As she did, she bumped into her father. She looked up at him. "Tomorrow," she said nodding and fled down the hallway.

"Peggy are you okay," he said after her and then turned to Orton "I don't know what's gotten into that..." He paused. "Oh no. Oh, good lord."

He wondered if it wasn't too late to send her to St. Theresa's Convent in Eau Claire. He had hoped it would have been another doctor or even the Lien kid, the lawyer's son who was planning on going to law school. Some cowboy from who knows where out west? He'd seen these nurse-patient romances before; usually they amounted to nothing. This one probably wouldn't either, but it would be a long three weeks and worth watching.

"Good night, Doc, and again thank you for everything," Orton said with a smile.

"Oh, you're welcome Mr. Orton. I'll look in on you in the morning but then I'll have to go to the hospital. I'll leave you in the care of Peggy," Sutter said and closed the door. Somehow, he had felt better leaving when Orton was in a coma.

Walking down the hallway on his way to his bedroom he saw the light on in his home office. Inside was Peggy, reading one of his books. "What are you doing, dear?" he asked.

"Going through your manual on physical rehabilitation," she said. "This will be the first time I have ever done anything like this. I hope you don't mind?"

Rather apprehensively, Sutter said, "By all means go ahead, but don't stay up too late." It was going to be a long three weeks.

In the morning Doc Sutter removed the bandages on Orton's feet. The stiches were holding, and the skin fold was beginning to heal into itself. He advised Peggy that each foot would have to be massaged for an hour to maintain circulation. He added that Orton's legs and arms also needed flexing.

"I know, Dad," she said. "Page 24 in the manual. I got it."

"Alright then, I'm headed for the hospital, will be back at five or so. Peggy, can you run down to my office and get my kit?" he asked.

As soon as she left. Sutter said to Orton, "Young man,

I want to remind you that this is my daughter, whom I care for very much. Do you understand?"

Orton nodded his head, "Yes sir, I do."

I'm hoping I won't hear those last two words of his anytime soon, Sutter thought. Peggy returned with the day kit. "By the way, how many eggs did Mr. Orton eat this morning? We seem to be almost out of the dozen I got yesterday."

"Six," she answered.

"Six?" he said.

Orton shrugged his shoulders and gave a half smile.

"I'll pick up six more dozen on the way home tonight along with a half a side of beef," Sutter said.

Over the days, a rhythm was established where Doc Sutter checked on Orton's feet and then Peggy took over with physical therapy. Each morning before leaving for school and each evening after school she massage both feet and then, with Orton's help, worked on his arms and legs. She would come home during her lunch hour and make her patient soup and sandwiches.

Orton was beginning to enjoy the attention, and seeing Peggy everyday eased the pain he felt in his amputated foot. Because of his made-up amnesia, he had no past to speak of. So he asked Peggy about hers. He found out her mother died at an early age and was raised by her father and a live-in nanny. The nanny left on Peggy's thirteenth birthday when the latter announced that she was now the woman of the house.

The aging nanny knew it, too. She had taught Peggy how to cook, sew, and look after a father who was always on the go with some emergency. Peggy also enjoyed reading her father's medical books. On weekends and occasionally after school, she would spend hours shadowing the nurses and doctors at the hospital. They found her and eager willing student. She let Orton know that she was planning to attend nursing school at the UW-Eau Claire State College after she graduated from high school in two years.

Orton began to notice how Peggy would purse her lips when she focused and squinted her eyes when she examined the stitches in his foot. He saw the bobbing of her blond curls in front of her small ears. He took the most delight in her smile when she looked up and found him looking at her. A smile he always returned. In the evening, when Doc Sutter checked on his condition, Peggy would come back to say good night. He would lie there and wait for sleep, so the morning could come, when he would see her again.

He knew that this warm feeling for her held dangers. She had a future. He had a past he could not forget that sometimes came back to him in vivid night dreams and a dread within the reality of what he had done to his father. Lurking in the greyness of his mind was the fact that Jack was out there, too, perhaps looking for him. All this because of what he had done to save the life of a girl much like Peggy. Yes, he had saved Peggy's life. Now Peggy was saving his.

Despite not being able to reveal his past, he wondered if someone like Peggy could love him anyway? Would the shadow of his secret self someday give the real Orton Wayland away? And when it did, would she or any other woman leave him in vile disgust?

Orton decided it could not happen. Regardless of what he felt for her, he would close the door to that love and get on with his life once he was able. His feet were getting better by the day. He would get a job in Hayward, pay off his debt to Doc Sutter and find his way to Detroit like he had planned. Peggy had her life; it was now up to him to find his own way. He would tell her his plans in the morning.

# 12

# TO THE RESCUE

As he awoke the next day Orton heard sirens. Police and ambulances were making their way south of the city as the blaring faded into the distance. Peggy came in, a wide-eyed look of concern on her face.

"What happened?" Orton asked?

"Dad got a call," she said. "He is on his way to the hospital. South of town on 63 a car collided with a school bus. He asked me to check on you and then stay here. They might need me at the hospital. How are you feeling?"

"I'm okay. No pain this morning."

"Well let's take a look." Peggy undid the bandage on his right foot. "This is looking a whole lot better. The swelling has gone down in your remaining toes and the amputation scar, while still stitched, has almost sealed itself."

The sirens returned. Peggy looked up and listened.

"Oh no, oh no," she said, "they are going back, that means multiple casualties." She went to work on massaging Orton's feet. They then went into the routine of working his limbs. The telephone down the hall rang. "Looks like I'll be leaving," she said.

Peggy ran down and grabbed the phone. Orton could hear her asking questions but could not quite make out the conversation. She returned a few minutes later.

"Jim, we have another emergency. That was Ed Bassett. His daughter has been in labor for 24 hours and is struggling. They are doing a home birth. Ed said there is a lot of bleeding and his wife Lydia, who is a midwife asked for an intervention. Normally Dad would go out and assist, but the hospital lines are jammed. I don't know what to do. I can't get a hold of the hospital either."

"Can you go out and help?" Orton asked.

"I could," she said, "but there is no way to get out there. Dad's got the car. Well, there is that old truck out back that a logger left for a bill payment, but that hasn't run for months."

"Did your dad take those rubber buckle boots with him?"

"No"

"Go get them."

"What?"

"Please do as I say," Orton demanded.

Peggy left and came back with the boots. Orton swung his legs off the bed and put his feet into the boots. He stood up unsteadily. "Help me take a few steps, I think I can do this."

"Jim, it's only been a week, you're not ready," she cried.

Orton put one hand on Peggy's shoulder and took a few steps out toward the door.

"I can do this," he said, "you go get what you need to help that poor girl. You are going to deliver a baby." Through a back window Orton spied the old truck. "I'll get that thing running." On his way he thought of how silly he must look in white hospital pajamas. He grabbed an old jacket off a rack and put on the black rubber boots.

Out at the truck, Orton tapped the gas tank and found it half full. Opening the driver's door, he chased several mice from the seat and hopped in. He cranked the throttle a quarter turn, pulled the choke all the way out, with a painful step on the gas pedal he turned the key. Dead. Orton got out and flipped the hood up. Corrosion or some critter had chewed the positive post copper wire at the battery almost off. Orton went back into the truck, found a penny that had been on the floor and went back to the engine. He jammed the coin into the battery connection and lay the remainder of the wire underneath it. A quick check of the engine told him this old jalopy should run.

Peggy arrived with a medical bag and got in the passenger's seat, or what was left of it.

"Will this thing run?" she asked.

"Maybe now," Orton announced as he turned the key and the engine sputtered and coughed itself to life. As it warmed, he adjusted the choke and throttle. "Go back inside and grab a blanket and one your dad's thicker warmer coats. There is no heater in this thing and this Wisconsin November of yours is colder than Montana." As soon as he said it, Orton winced. Rats, he said to himself. He knew he would have to be more careful, or he would give his past away.

"You're from Montana? You remembered that!" Peggy said leaving for the house. She came right back with the coat and blanket. Orton put the coat on over the light one he had on, and Peggy put the blanket between them.

"I must have heard that expression 'colder than a Montana winter' from somewhere," Orton said.

"How did you get this thing going?" she asked.

As they pulled out of the driveway he said, "You can thank Mr. Lincoln. Now which way?"

"Take a left on 63 here and then a right on 70. We then go five or six more miles to a gravel road," she instructed. "Lincoln, like Abe Lincoln, is that what you said?"

While Orton drove, he took note of the pinging sound of the little four-cylinder engine. Something wasn't right.

He adjusted the choke which helped. As long as he could keep it running, he felt he could get Peggy to her waiting patient. The truck was a 1928 model A Ford, several of which Orton had worked on at Harshaw's garage in Montana. This was the first series that had a carburetor atop the engine. Orton knew they could be finicky and always needed adjustment.

"How do you know where this place is?" he asked.

"Dad and I had to come out here two summers ago," she said. "The same woman who needs us now had caught her arm in a combine. Dad and Mr. Bassett got her out of it about the time the ambulance arrived. They managed to save the arm but only after a long time in surgery at the hospital."

A late morning sun crept into the truck's cab and helped warm Orton's fingers as they gripped the steering wheel. Occasionally, he tucked one hand underneath the blanket to warm it. When it came time to warm his right hand, he found Peggy's hand. She gripped it.

"Jim, your hand is cold. I should have grabbed some of dad's gloves too. How does your foot feel?"

"I'm fine, I'll be okay," he said, even though he gritted his teeth every time he pressed his foot hard on the gas pedal. "How much further?"

"About another mile and just past a big white pine we turn onto a dirt road," she said. "We should be there in a few minutes."

Something else bothered Orton, but he couldn't quite figure out what it was. The world seemed to be pressing in on him. He felt claustrophobic, like he was driving down a tunnel that kept closing in. Then he realized he was not used to being hemmed in by trees, trees everywhere. This was a land of forests with a few scattered farms. In Montana, the world was wide open -- where a person could see for 50 miles in any direction. He laughed to himself.

"What's so funny?" Peggy asked.

"Oh, my left foot itches," he said. "Is that the turn off by the big fuzzy green tree?"

"Yeah, that's it. About a half mile on the right, turn into the farmyard."

Ed Bassett, a short heavy-set man in bib overalls with a worried look, met Orton and Peggy at the door and took Peggy to the bedroom. His wife Lydia attended their daughter Anne at her bedside. Her eyes were closed, and she was breathing rapidly.

"Annie, it's me, Peggy Sutter. I want to...."

"Momma another one's comin' on, Momma hold my hand, Momma it hurts," Anne sat up and her back stiffened, her face was a grimace of immense pain. She screamed out.

Peggy in a loud voice said, "Anne can you bear down at all?"

Anne gave no response; she only screamed louder.

Peggy opened the bedsheets and found Anne had only dilated a few centimeters in 20 hours of labor. The sheets below Anne were stained with blood.

"Lydia, how often have you changed these sheets?" Peggy asked.

"Three times!"

"How long have the contractions been going on?"

"Since last night at about four. They are now 15 minutes apart and it doesn't seem like that baby wants to arrive yet."

"We have to start massaging the uterus. You work on the left and I'll take the right. We've got to get that bleeding to stop, and I hope we can stretch the area there to allow that baby to come out. First, I've got to run some tests." Peggy went to work. Using some fresh blood, she checked the white blood cell count and found it low. Anne's pulse was irregular, and her face was grey. Peggy was afraid this mother couldn't handle too many more contractions.

"We have got to get more fluids into this woman," Peggy said. "Lydia, have you got any herbal teas."

"I've got some sumac tea; would that help?"

"Yes, have Mr. Bassett make a quart of it."

While Lydia was gone to her husband with instructions to make tea, Anne had another convulsive contraction. Peggy noticed more bleeding. A fear began to rise in the young nurse. This woman needed blood, or she and the baby would die. She'd lost too much already. She needed blood and without it she'd go into hypovolemic shock and the baby would not get enough oxygen.

When Lydia returned, Peggy asked her what blood type she and her husband were. Lydia said she had no idea. What Peggy did know was Anne had A positive blood based on her surgery from two years ago. Neither parent could give blood without endangering the life of their daughter. Then Peggy remembered, Jim Orton's blood is A positive. He could safely give.

Peggy left Lydia after telling her how to massage the uterus. She found Orton in a chair talking to Ed in the living room. She got close, bent over and looked directly into Orton's eyes.

"Jim, I need you. I need you to give some of your blood to Anne. She has lost a lot of blood and there is no way to get her to the hospital. We need it now or we might lose her and the baby. I know you have been through a lot these past couple of weeks, but I feel you are strong enough to do this. Would you be willing?"

Orton stood up. His eyes were wide, and he stared at Peggy.

"You need my blood, but how?"

"We will put you on another bed close to Anne. I've two IV needles and a long rubber tube and we can transfer your blood directly into her body."

Orton nodded. "Yes, okay let's go."

Ed Bassett retrieved a cot from his storage room. He put it in the bedroom next to Anne's bed. Within a few minutes Peggy inserted a needle into Orton's arm and then inserted another needle attached to the rubber tube into Anne's arm. Anne was too weak to protest. She obeyed all the orders directed her way. As another contraction came and went, it frightened Orton who had never been through anything like this. It was all he could do to keep himself together for Peggy's sake.

Peggy monitored the blood flow and massaged Anne, taking over for Lydia who stood up exhausted. She had not slept in 24 hours.

"Ma'am," Orton whispered to Lydia. "I've a bit of a strange request. I remember my mom used to sing to me to help calm me down, and I'd sure appreciate if you could sing to me now. Just one song, please."

"Sure Mr. Orton," Lydia said, "was there a special song you had in mind?"

"My favorite was Amazing Grace."

Lydia in a soft soprano voice began to sing. Orton closed his eyes and smiled, relaxing for the first time that day. Outside a half open door, Ed Bassett heard it to. With tears in his eyes, he also began to sing along with his wife.

".... how sweet the sound that saved and set me free...."

As another contraction came on Anne heard the singing, too. "Daddy," she said, "Daddy." And without a scream she held her breath and bore down hard and the baby came out, much to the surprise of a young nurse down below who caught it. As the singing stopped, a baby began to cry.

Peggy cleaned the baby and clipped the umbilical cord.

"Lydia, quick take the baby," Peggy said. In the excitement she had forgotten about Orton.

When Lydia took the new infant and wrapped it in a soft cotton blanket, Peggy withdrew the needle from Orton's arm and then Anne's. She then bandaged and taped both arms. Anne lay back in the bed with a smile on her face and waved to her mother to bring the baby to her.

Orton opened his eyes. "The baby?" he asked. "Did I have a baby?" And he closed his eyes again.

"I think Mr. Orton gave too much of his blood to Anne," Peggy laughed. "He'll be okay. We'll let him sleep for a while to get his strength back." Peggy saw that the baby was happily in its mother's arms. Ed Bassett and his wife were on each side of her admiring their new granddaughter.

Peggy remembered Orton's foot. She pulled off the buckle boot and found his bandages stained with blood. Lydia saw it too.

"What is that?" she asked.

"This guy, this guy I'll tell ya," Peggy explained, "some of his stitches in his foot must have ripped when he drove us over here. He said he was fine, but it must have been painful. I knew he wasn't ready yet, but do you think this man would listen to me. He insisted. Wait until the doctor sees what happened to his nice stitching. I hope I'm not around when he sees this."

Peggy took the old bandages off and replaced them with new ones she had in her kit. When done, she took his wrist and checked his pulse. It was in the normal range. She couldn't put his arm down. Instead, she took hold of his hand and gave it a little squeeze. The hand squeezed back. They looked at each other and smiled.

This touch from her, thought Orton through a fuzzy haze, was different than any other he had felt from her in the past week. This touch said I care for your heart and soul. This touch said hold me and do not let go. In an instant all thoughts of leaving Hayward and going to Detroit began to vanish. By this simple touch of her hand on his, Orton knew that he was bound to her forever.

"How do you feel," Peggy asked?

"A little dizzy," he replied, "and thirsty."

Lydia got up and headed for the door. "I'll get him some of that sumac tea," she said.

"Put some sugar in it," Peggy said.

"I'll do one better. I've got some honey Ed made and

I'll add some of that," said Lydia as she started to leave.

"Wait a minute," Orton said and looked over at Anne and the baby. "Miss Anne would probably like some, too, wouldn't you?"

"Why, yes I would," said Anne, "I think I could drink the well dry." Lydia nodded a smile and left.

Ed Bassett looked at Orton who had returned his gaze to Peggy. Amazing, he thought. Here was a young man he never knew who, despite his own pain, drove medical help to his daughter, gave his own blood to save her life and is now watching after her. Bassett looked at his daughter and granddaughter and knew what he had to do.

Lydia came back and gave a warm mug of tea to Orton. She set Anne's tea down next to her.

"Anne, darling," she said, "you have to give me the baby while you drink." Reluctantly, Anne handed the bundle to her mother. Ed Bassett put an arm around the two of them and said, "Lydia, Anne, I have a request and I hope you will honor me with it. I'd like to name this little girl Jamie, after Mr. Orton here. I'm not sure but that without his help all this wouldn't be possible." Tears streaked the older man's cheeks.

"Oh daddy," Anne said, "you're right. Yes, Jamie Lydia Nordstrom. That's it. And to think Phillip and I had a dozen boy-girl names that just didn't seem to fit. Jamie Lydia Nordstrom. I like it."

Lydia smiled and gently rocked the sleeping baby in her arms, "I like it, too."

Orton coughed up some of his drink in surprise. "Hey, don't I have any say in this?" he asked.

The three others in the room looked at him and said an affirmative "No."

"And, Mr. Orton," Ed said, "in a few months when we have Jamie baptized at our church, we'd be grateful if you would be there. You,too, Peggy."

"Yes, Mr. Bassett, I will be there," Orton said.

"As will I," Peggy added.

With that the door to Detroit shut forever.

Two hours later, Phillip Nordstrom came busting in through the doors. His tie hung wildly out from his vested suit, and he quickly shook off his coat. "Where is she?" he said to a startled Ed and Jim standing in the living room.

"You will find your new daughter and wife in the back· bedroom," Bassett said.

Phillip disappeared down the hall. While he was gone, Ed explained to Orton that the baby was two weeks early. Phillip was a salesman for a farm implement company, and sales had been going well. Bassett had put in several calls to various dealers that Nordstrom might call on. He had been expected to be away for several days.

Nordstrom later walked into the living room excited. "She's beautiful," he said, "absolutely beautiful. I don't believe it. Mr. Orton, the girls told me the whole story, and I own you a debt of thanks and am proud to have my daughter named after you." He shook Orton's hand.

Orton blushed a bit and said, "You are welcome; glad I could be of help."

"Where did they catch up to you?" Bassett asked.

"I was selling in the Eau Claire area this morning, so I thought I'd stop in the district office and see Harlan," Nordstrom said. "As soon as I walked in, Harlan gave me a box of cigars and said to me 'Here take these, son; you're going to need them.' I said 'What?' And he told me about your phone call, dad. I told Harlan Anne wasn't due for two weeks yet, and he shoved the cigars and me out the door."

Orton and Bassett laughed. Then the three of them stood in silence for a few minutes. Finally, Bassett said, "So where are those damn cigars?"

The mid November night was closing in when Peggy Sutter finally got through to the hospital in Hayward. The nurse at the other end of the line said her father had sent a car to the house late morning to pick Peggy up as they needed her at the hospital. The driver returned and said she and a Mr. Orton were gone. Her dad was furious. Peggy found out, too, that her dad was back in surgery with another accident victim and was expected home about midnight. Peggy left a message for her dad saying she and Jim were okay and that they would see him at the house about the same time and not to worry, she would explain everything.

Orton limped into Peggy's home hallway and sat down on the deacon's bench. He was tired and his foot ached. Peggy came through the door shortly behind him about the same time her father charged out of his office. He looked at the two of them in a rage.

"How far did you get before that damned ol' truck broke down? Madison, Duluth, St. Paul? Where in the hell were you going?" Sutter looked at Orton and lowered his finger. "And to think I trusted you, son. I want you out...."

Ed Bassett did a quick knock at the door and came in. "Peggy," he said, "I found your stethoscope on the car floor, it must have dropped out of your bag, thought you might need it." He looked up and saw Sutter. "Oh, hi Doc. You can be proud of this daughter of yours. She delivered Anne's baby after getting some bleeding stopped." Nodding at Orton he said, "And that young man, THAT young man saved Anne's and the baby's life. Doc, I'm a grand pa thanks to these two."

Sutter's face turned into a wrinkled puzzle. "What, Ed, what are you talking about?"

Bassett looked at Sutter. "Of course, they didn't have time to tell you, Doc. Anne went into labor yesterday afternoon. Lydia, who you know has helped deliver more than a few babies, thought she could handle it on her own. But this morning the baby hadn't come, and Anne was beginning to bleed so we called the hospital but couldn't get through. Then we called you here and Peggy answered. She told us about the bus accident and that you and the ambulances would be tied up for a while. So, this young man, from what I later found out, got an old truck running and, despite ripping stiches in his foot, drove Peggy to my place. Well, Peggy got the bleeding stopped but Anne needed blood. Peggy knew for certain that Anne and Jim's blood were a match, so his blood was transferred directly into Anne's arm."

Sutter interrupted, "Peggy, you did a direct line?"

Peggy nodded, "Yes, I read how to do it months ago in one of your books."

Sutter put his hand to his chin and looked at the floor. "Unbelievable'" he smiled, "unbelievable."

Bassett continued. "Jim almost passed out, too; apparently he gave Anne too much blood."

"Dad, it was hard to gauge," Peggy cut in, "and I was watching the baby's progress."

Sutter looked at Orton. "How do you feel now Jim?"

"Okay, I'm fine.... maybe a little tired."

"And that foot of yours, you ripped my stiches didn't you, and it must be painful now isn't it?"

Orton looked at Peggy. "She rewrapped it; it's fine."

"Dad", Peggy said, "it needs to be restitched, it's still bleeding a little."

"Jim," Sutter said raising his voice, "does that foot hurt? Tell me the truth!"

Orton looked directly into Sutter's eyes and said, "Yes sir, it hurts bad."

In a quieter voice Sutter said, "Jim, go down to your bedroom and get into the bed. I and your nurse here will be down in a few minutes to restitch that foot, a foot you are to stay off of for the next two weeks. Got it?"

Orton nodded and hobbled down the hall to his room. Peggy left to get antiseptic, gloves, a needle, and stitching thread.

Sutter turned to Bassett and laughingly said, "Ed, you may have saved these two peoples' life."

"What?" Bassett asked.

"Before you came in, I was getting ready to read those two the riot act. I thought they had eloped and run off, thinking maybe that old truck had broke down somewhere and they came home. I know those two are kind of sweet on each other. Where is that old truck now by the way?"

"It's at my place," Bassett said. "Jim was going to drive it back tonight, but Peggy and Lydia said absolutely not," and laughing hard he continued. "Poor Jim realized he couldn't fight two women. Anyway, Phil came back early so I used the car and brought them both back here. Say, I need you to write me up a bill for the delivery. Oh, and Phil and I can drive that truck back tomorrow afternoon."

"Don't worry about that baby's bill," Sutter said, "and as for that truck maybe you'd better keep it until you get yours fixed. I'd feel better if young Mr. Orton didn't have wheels." He laughed. "Unbelievable. Can you bring the baby by the hospital in a few days for a checkup? How are Anne and the baby doing?"

"Fine," Bassett said. "Peggy checked them both out and they are doing great. He reached into his pocket and pulled out a cigar. "Here, I almost forgot to give you one of these."

Sutter took the cigar. "Thanks. What is the name of this little girl?"

"Jamie Lydia."

"Jamie?"

"After Mr. Orton," Bassett said proudly.

"Unbelievable!"

"You'd better see to your patient before he bleeds to death," Bassett said, shaking Sutter's hand and heading for the door.

After Bassett left, Sutter stood in the hallway looking at the closed door. He took in all the events that happened at the hospital that day. In surgery he had saved the lives of two children involved in the bus accident and set broken bones on two more. He failed to save the life of the driver of the car who had hit the bus.

As he cleaned and washed his hands getting ready to restitch Orton's foot, he looked into the bathroom mirror. "Unbelievable", he said shaking his head as he thought about what his daughter and Orton must have gone through.

After he and Peggy had resewn Orton's foot, he watched as Peggy gently wrapped the bandages. He noticed, too, Jim's nervous loving glances toward Peggy, and Peggy catching them like two people discreetly tossing a ball back and forth.

"Well, I'm done, "Sutter said, "and I am going to bed. He stopped at Orton's bedside.

"Jim".

"Yes, sir."

"Have you kissed my daughter yet?" he asked aloud.

Orton's eyes grew wide with a hint of fear.

"No, sir; no, sir, I haven't."

"And why the hell not? Is there anything wrong with her?"

Peggy stopped bandaging and smiled. Sutter heel turned and walked out the door.

"What, what was that all about?" Orton asked.

Feeling as happy as she had ever been, she continued wrapping Orton's foot.

"Your doctor has given his permission for you to fraternize with your nurse," she said with a grin.

"Oh, fraternize... fraternize?" Orton said thinking

hard and laid his head back down on the pillow and gazed at the ceiling. Then he quickly snapped it back up and looked at Peggy in a wide beam smile, saying "Ooooooooooh."

# 13

# TOGETHER

THE NEXT TWO WEEKS WENT BY MUCH LIKE THE FIRST. IN the mornings, Peggy would unwrap the foot and check the progress of its healing. She would massage it, do physical therapy on Orton's legs and arms, and then give him a quick kiss as she left for school. At noon hour break, she came home and made him soup. They talked about her day and her classes. Before leaving for school, she would kiss him again. The hours between their meetings would drag into eternity. When she came home, Orton would hear her enter the door and follow her progress through the house to his room. When the door opened his life began anew.

Once in mid-week, Sutter came home for lunch. The three of them enjoyed soup and sandwiches in Orton's room. The doctor checked his watch and said he wanted to leave, so Peggy would have some privacy to kiss Orton goodbye.

"Daddy," she said, "have you been spying on us?"

Sutter was bemused that he caught her admitting to something he had suspected. "No," he said, "but I was young once a time ago and I remember a woman who kissed me a few times until I couldn't live without her." He winked at Orton. "See you two tonight." He left them alone.

"Can you tell me what happened to your mother?" Orton asked.

"Only from what daddy told me. She died from a rare nerve disease. Daddy did everything medically he could be it was not enough. He took her to St. Paul to a big hospital there, but nothing helped. I was only two years old. Dad got a nanny to take care of me who lived with us after mom passed. Dad said mom was not in any pain, but he lied about that. I got a hold of her medical records. With tears in her eyes, she continued. "Mom was in pain, and they had to give her morphine constantly."

Orton drew her close and took her hands in his. "It's not hereditary, is it?" he asked.

"Thank God, no," she said. He pulled her close and kissed her.

"You'd better go. I don't want you to be late for your one o'clock."

She reached into her school bag. "Here are a few more

westerns. One by a guy named Zane Grey I think you'd like. And I got a couple on fixing cars and trucks that you asked for. The school librarian lets me take as many books as I want as long as they are for patients. Besides, the way you go through these books, I never have to worry about getting them back late."

The books she brought from the school library passed the time while she was at school. Orton was enjoying this little vacation and knew it would unfortunately end when his foot healed. He had no clue as to what he would do once he could safely walk again. The answer to that mystery ended a few days later one morning after Peggy left. Doc Sutter came into his room with a man who was introduced as the high school guidance counselor. Carried with him were ability tests. For the next three hours Orton was tested on mathematics, English, history, geography, biology, and civics.

Peggy came in at noon. "Mr. Falk, Daddy said you'd be stopping by, but I thought that was next week."

"Your dad wants your patient here to start the spring semester," Falk explained, "Because of Orton's amnesia, we don't know what grade to put him in; so we have to test. By the looks of these answers this morning, we could, with your tutoring, start him as a junior. He has got excellent reading and math skills, but his grammar and biology need work. The remainder is about average." Falk looked at Orton. "Young man, have you any recollection of what grade you were in or where you went to school?"

Orton lied. "No sir, I do not remember." In reality, Orton learned math while working on cars and trucks in Harshaws' garage, as a necessary skill to calibrate brakes and engine parts. Reading he took to naturally at an early age as he had enjoyed being read to by his mother who had also encouraged Orton to study hard. After he entered his junior year in Livingstone, he was pulled out of school when his dad took him and Jack to the Missouri Breaks for the ill-fated hostage crime.

As he thought about the Breaks, the voice of his father filled his being. "I'm coming back for you boy. I'm here in the sand of this river, but it won't hold me forever." Orton gripped tightly the sheets of the bed. His teeth clenched and his body shook.

"Jim, Jim," Peggy yelled, "Jim what's the matter? Jim."

The guidance counselor grabbed Orton by the shoulder and when he did Orton fisted his left hand and began to swing it into the face of his father. Then he stopped himself; his breathing was heavy. Sweat trickled down his face. He lay back in the bed remembering now where he was. He saw Peggy's frightened face looking at him.

She grabbed his wrist. "Your heart, your pulse, I've never seen it this high. Jim, lay back, be quiet, it is okay."

She looked at Falk and steered him into the hallway. As she left, she said, "Jim I'll be right back."

Down the hall out of earshot she told Falk, "Mr. Orton has been through a traumatic experience. We don't know why or how and he cannot recall any of it. We do know that sometimes in the night he has nightmares and calls out for a guy named Wayland. Sometimes he says a man named Jack is coming. It could be those men who beat him up and put him on that rail car. We don't know."

Falk asked, "He's not dangerous, is he?"

"Oh no, I think Mr. Orton is one of the gentlest boys I've ever known. Something is haunting his past, and I am hoping that once we get him in a normal social setting like school again, he'll regain a sense of self and purpose."

"Peggy, Mr. Falk?" Orton was calling from his room.

The two returned to Orton. "Mr. Falk, forgive me. I meant you no harm. I don't know what came over me. I want to thank you for all your time this morning, and I look forward to starting school in January. Any other schoolbooks you can pass along my way to help before that time I would appreciate it."

Falk smiled, "It's okay Mr. Orton. Peggy said you have been through a bit of an ordeal, and I am willing to help see you through it, too. If you ever want to talk to me about anything let me know."

"Thank you, sir," Orton said.

Falk then said to Peggy, "I can see my way out. I'll tell

Miss Olson you may be a few minutes late."

"Oh, and Mr. Falk, I'd have your mechanic to check the carburetor on that new chevy truck of yours. That sounds like the problem with the chugging you feel," Orton said.

"Alright kid, thanks," Falk said, "I'll have him look at it." Falk left.

"I thought you guys were testing for math and English. What's this carburetor thing?"

"He'd heard about my fixing that old logger's truck, so he asked me about a problem he was having with a new truck he bought. He going to enroll me into a shop mech class. Soooo, Miss Sutter, can I carry your books to school for you?"

"No, I am going to be carrying yours. You're going to be on crutches for the next two months."

"Well then why don't you carry me, too?"

"Oh, good lord, I've got to go."

Peggy turned to leave. Orton called out. "Nurse, aren't you forgetting something? My lips hurt."

She came back and gave him a light kiss. "You are hopeless."

"I think you mean helpless."

"Both," she said and was gone.

Doc Sutter noticed a new sense of happiness about his daughter. One he had never seen. While she had always treated him with love and respect, she now went through her day with a new lightness of being. She was more attentive to his needs when he came home after a particularly trying day at the hospital, and she would put her arms around him and give him a light kiss on his cheek, set him down in his chair, and get him some tea. So, too, with a touch of joy and sadness, he realized she was changing more and more into a woman. This child of his he knew would someday leave this house and probably join Mr. Orton in their own home, hopefully nearby.

He remembered the wife he had lost many years ago, a loss he never fully got over. He had pictures of his lovely Mary in his office at the hospital and at his home, constant reminders of a love he had once known. After Mary died, he threw all of his energy into his work and bringing up his little girl. He was smart enough to know he couldn't hang onto Peggy forever and that someday his life would change. He would come home to an empty house. It all seemed so unreal. For now, he was enjoying his daughter's newfound love with Orton and some of that joy was beginning to rub off on him. He began to take more pleasure in the advances of a widowed nurse who coincidently found time to have coffee with him in the cafeteria. Perhaps, he might someday ask her out for dinner. He was hoping to find out more about her son who had recently enlisted in the army as part of a call to arms by President Roosevelt. A mad man name Adolf

Hitler, along with his minions, had invaded Poland and threatened another world war in Europe. There were also reports from the South Pacific of a growing Japanese empire. Unbelievable, Sutter thought, unbelievable.

Peggy Sutter and Jim Orton graduated from high school in May 1941. Jim immediately started working for Ford motors in Hayward as a full-time mechanic following the endorsement of the school shop teacher. As a graduation present, Doc Sutter gave Orton the keys to the old truck that the latter had been fixing up anyway for the past year and half. That truck now had a working heater and a new transmission. The carburetor, however, needed constant adjustment.

Peggy took a job with the hospital as an assistant to a nurse in the emergency room. Occasionally she would join her dad and his new friend Alice for lunch breaks in the cafeteria. Talk usually centered around Peggy's preparation for the two-year nursing college in Eau Claire where she would start in September.

Doc Sutter never sent a bill to the Bassett-Nordstrom family for the delivery of baby Jamie. However, every market Monday, free eggs and a gallon of fresh milk always found its way to the Sutter refrigerator along with a loaf of homemade bread. And it was usually two dozen eggs to make up for Orton's healthy appetite.

Jim picked up his dozen on his way home from work and took them to his apartment. After his foot healed in

December, he found a cheap room a few blocks from the Sutters. He had managed to pay his way through odd jobs working on cars and as a janitor at the county office building. Doc Sutter insisted that he join them each evening for dinner and often joined, too, by Doc's new nurse friend.

Peggy and Jim agreed that any talk of marriage would take place after she graduated from nursing school. Jim also wanted time to work and save enough money for a house. When alone, Peggy sometimes let slip her intentions with questions like, "Jim how many children would you like to have if you were married?"

Jim would answer: "Gee, I dunno. I didn't think we'd talk about this until after you graduated."

And she would say in a high disappointed pitch, "Mr. Orton, haven't you thought about us at all?"

In reply he'd say, "Well yeah, but not about children, geez."

It ended when Jim gave in to as many children, gardens, chickens, and new appliances Peggy wanted. That, along with a long kiss, and a warm "I love you." Peggy was happy with the way the conversations started and ended knowing it would give Jim something to think about when she was away in school.

Doc Sutter and Jim took Peggy and all her needed clothes and school supplies to Eau Claire on the first day of September. It was the end of the most wonder filled summer Jim had ever known,     interrupted only by nightmares of a dead father that came back to haunt him in his dreams and at times in conscious memories of what he had done. Most of the time he put those evil thoughts out of his mind, and they disappeared the moment he saw and held Peggy in his arms. Now she would be gone until Thanksgiving and later Christmas break. He was afraid that without her the demon would return more often. With that he wrote her a letter every day, which he brought into the local post office on his way to work. The clerks and carriers knew him by name.

The school semester passed, and Jim was saddened to hear that Peggy intended to stay in Eau Claire that summer going to school in preparation for an advanced degree. As often as he could, he drove the old truck the 85 miles to spend a Saturday or Sunday with her. He longed for the day he could pick her up and take her home one last time. Unbeknownst to her, he found a small house on the south end of town along the Namekagon River. He was negotiating with a realtor to buy it.

On a cool crisp and clear day in early December 1941, Jim drove a new car into the showroom. The place was empty. Odd, he thought. Where were the dealers and the customers?  Going into a back room, he found all the employees and a few clients huddled around a radio. An announcement was in progress by President Roosevelt that the Japanese had attacked a place called Pearl

Harbor in Hawaii. War was declared on Japan and Germany. The men's faces showed anger and revulsion.

"The dirty slant eyed bastards," said one.

"And I can't wait to get my hands on that little black mustached asshole in Germany, too," said another.

The car dealers' manager with disgust said, "With all the steel and iron going into constructing tanks and bombs, I don't think we will be making or selling many more cars for a while."

A slightly older woman, the company's secretary typist who had two sons working as loggers, shook her head and wept.

With America now committed to another foreign war, a nationwide draft began a call up of men. The first to go were the sons of the company's secretary whose father had been wounded in France in the first world war. Many more men in the Hayward area enlisted. Despite a plea from his wife not to go, Phillip Nordstrom joined the army. Another enlistee was Harry Whitman, a rural route mail man.

As Orton entered the post office one morning to send his daily letter to Peggy, he was stopped by the postmaster Zack Cohen.

"Jim, can I see you in my office for a minute?" he asked.

"Sure Mr. Cohen," Jim replied and followed him into an office off a hallway.

"Take a seat there; can I get you coffee?"

"No sir, I'm fine."

"Jim, with Harry Whitman going soon I am short a driver for route two and I was hoping you could take it until Harry comes back. It would be substitute pay, but I believe it would be twice what you are getting paid now at the car dealer. The job would be yours until Harry returns, and when that happens, I think I could find you full time work here when some of our older guys retire. Not sure how long this damn war is going to last. I understand you have been down to the draft board?"

"Yes, sir, but because of my foot they rejected me. I asked them to take me, and I showed them how well I could walk and told them I could drive. I even offered to take a desk job somewhere, but they still wouldn't take me." Sadly, Jim looked down at the floor.

"Well, I tell you son, the postmaster said, "delivering mail is a darned important job to the American people, and you'd be doing a service to your country by filling this route. What do you say?  Harry's not leaving for two weeks, and he said he could train a replacement in one."

Orton looked up at the postmaster; the world suddenly seemed a little brighter. Only yesterday the car company had cut his hours due to a lack of business. He was going to talk to the realtor today and tell them that he wouldn't be able to buy the house on the river. The prospect of getting that house now seemed within reach.

"Okay, yes," Orton stood up and put his hand out to Cohen. "I'd be honored to help you out."

Cohen stood and shook Orton's hand. "Glad to have you on son. I was hoping you could help us. I'll talk to your boss at the car dealer and tell him what's going on. Harry can start training you on Wednesday. You'll be on the payroll starting then. Harry says you can use his car for deliveries until he gets back as we pay a good mileage allotment on personal vehicles. Because of that allotment, most of our guys get new cars ever couple of years."

Orton left the post office without sending Peggy's letter. Instead, he went back to his apartment and wrote a new one telling her about the post office job. He did not tell her he was about to buy a house. That evening, Orton went to Doc Sutter's house and formally asked permission to marry his daughter.

"I was wondering when this day would come, and I'm not surprised since I helped things along. I also know there is only one man in this world Peggy wants to marry and that is you." Sutter said. "By the way, you wouldn't mind if Alice and I make your wedding arrangements, would you? I think we can plan a pretty special day. But let's keep this between us."

On May 25, 1943, Peggy Sutter, in cap and gown, walked up and received her nursing certificate on graduation day in Eau Claire. She was second in her class behind her best friend Sally Yeazle. Sally had given the commencement address. In the crowd was a misty-eyed doctor and a young mailman wearing a brand-new suit and tie.

After the ceremony, Doc Sutter gave his daughter a big hug. Orton did the same, followed by a quick kiss on her lips. The elder Sutter then disappeared.

"Where did Daddy go?" Peggy asked.

"Oh, he had business elsewhere. He said he'd meet us later for dinner at his house. I'm to take you back in the old truck. Are you ready to go?"

"Yes, my suitcases are at Schofield Hall but I need to say goodbye to Sally," she said looking around through the throng of students, parents and teachers. She spied Sally's parents.

"Mr. and Mrs. Yeazle, where is Sally?" she asked.

"Oh dear," Mrs. Yeazle replied, "I'm sorry you just missed her. Sally had to go and see some friends out of town." Over their shoulder Mr. Yeazle gave Orton a big wink. Orton, with a smile, winked back.

"Jim, could you help Peggy out of the graduation gown?" And to Peggy she said, "Sally told me Doc Sutter bought you a beautiful dress for this day."

Jim helped Peggy out of the gown and then he tucked it under his arm. Underneath the gown was a satin frilled white dress. Peggy stood out from the other girls in the room. Many stopped and admired the dress.

"Daddy was adamant that I wear this today," Peggy

said with a wrinkled brow. "He was kind of funny about the whole thing. Something about a fathers' special request. I dunno...." She shrugged her shoulders.

Minutes later, after a few more goodbyes and picking up suitcases, Jim had Peggy on her way up Highway 53 to Hayward. The day was bright, sunny, and warm. The two hours travel time went by quickly. They rolled into Hayward.

"Hey, you goof ball. We passed daddy's street. Where are you taking me?"

"Just hold on," Orton said. Two blocks more and they pulled into a vacant area in front of a church. The parking lot was full of cars and trucks. "I forgot to tell you; your dad is getting married today."

He got out of the car and helped her out. Peggy was angry.

"You and daddy can't pull this kind of surprise on me. I knew dad and Alice were close, but you should have told me. This is one big day for them to pull this off on my graduation day! No wonder he wanted me to wear this dress. I suppose I'm one of the bridesmaids?"

They opened the church doors and walked in. The congregation turned, looked at them, and stood up. At the altar stood Alice and Sally Yeazle.

Without thinking, Peggy said out loud "Yeazy what are you doing here?" Sally, in a dress similar to the one Peggy was wearing, only smiled. "Oh, oh," and Peggy, with this new discovery, began to cry. Orton left her and walked to the altar. Out of nowhere, Doc Sutter appeared and took the stunned young bride-to-be by the arm. As they walked the aisle, Peggy whispered to her father.

"He's never lied to me, but Jim said you were getting married today."

"I am," he said, "and so are you."

Zach Cohen was Jim's best man. Sally was the maid of honor. Jim served as Doc Sutter's best man with Peggy as Alice's maid of honor. Two-and-a-half-year-old Jamie Nordstrom stood by with two rings in her tiny little hands.

For years people would talk about this joyous wedding. It seemed most of Hayward turned out for the occasion as the Sutters had many friends in and outside of town. Amidst the toasts, food and dancing the gloom of war was forgotten.

# 14

# WAR MAIL

THE WAR, HOWEVER, WENT ON. AFTER A 3-DAY HONEYMOON to Bayfield, Wisconsin, Peggy took a job that was waiting for her at the hospital, and Orton returned to his mail route. Each day he delivered letters from sons to mothers and husbands to wives from far away battlefields. At times, these women would be waiting at the mailbox for the next letter to arrive. Orton would hand them the mail, talk briefly, and drive on.

Marilyn Little Crow waited one morning for Orton. Orton stopped.

"Nothing today again," Orton said.

"Are you sure?" she asked, "Henry has been so good with his letters."

"I'm sure they'll come. Sometimes when those armies are on the move it takes a while for that mail to catch up.

I've seen it before." He drove on.

Two days later a telegram letter in Army stationary was handed to Marilyn. With Orton looking on she tore open the letter, read a few lines and dropped to her knees weeping. Orton got out of the car.

"Marilyn, what happened?"

She handed him the letter. In a few lines it read, "Mrs. Little Crow. It is with deep regret to inform you that your husband Henry has been killed in action in Tunisia. Please accept our deepest sympathies. His personal effects will be sent to you in a few weeks. Sincerely, the U.S. Department of the Army."

"Oh, Marilyn, I am so sorry," Orton said, "let me help you up and get you into your house."

"No, please Jim," she said, "leave me here and take this letter back with you. I'm sure my Henry will be sending me more letters. I'll just wait here until they come. Henry is okay, he's okay, he'll write me again."

"Marilyn, you cannot sit out here in the hot sun with all these mosquitoes and black flies. Why don't you go into the house, and I'll honk my horn when I have Henry's letters? Okay?"

Orton helped the young woman up and walked her into her house and to a living room chair. On a bookshelf, in the dimly lit room, Orton saw pictures of two young smiling couples in a wedding dress and suit and photographs, too, of Henry smartly dressed in his army uniform looking strong and confident.

"Marilyn," Orton commanded, "stay here until I get another letter from Henry. Okay?"

The young woman gazed out the window into the early summer morning. She nodded her head in agreement and smiled.

As he left her, returning to his car, it crossed Orton's mind that that could have been Peggy getting a letter from the Army about him. He quickly tossed the thought out of his head. A few houses down and Orton went into the home of Emma Isham. This elderly woman had been a midwife to many mothers in the area and had helped deliver Marilyn and Henry. Her wrinkled face belied years of working farm fields in the summer warmth and making wild rice in the autumn cool. Her thinning silver white hair matted down her small back.

Before Orton could speak, Emma Isham said, "Mr. Orton I fear our Henry is dead. I'll go over and help Marilyn. It will take time. Much time. Those two were so much in love. From my window here I watched you take her into the house and knew from the way she walked that a part of her was now gone. Thank you for stopping by. I'll take it from here."

Relieved of not having to give the explanation, Orton nodded to the elder, returned to his car and finished his route. Getting back to the post office, he looked into his empty mail slots and thought of how many more of the

Army's telegram letters, like the one addressed to Marilyn Little Crow, would he have to deliver. Fixing cars was easier.

That night, in bed with Peggy, the horrid dream of his dead father returned. Jim Orton and Carl Wayland were on a desert battlefield in North Africa. The two men were fighting with broad swords. While Jim feared for his life, his father laughed and danced around him, taking menacing swipes with the long blade. Over and over again his father kept saying, "the Germans or Japanese may not get you boy, but I will."

Peggy woke him up. "Jim, Jim, it's okay you're having that dream again."

He opened his eyes and looked at Peggy. "What happened?"

"You're having those dreams again. Who is Wayland and Jack and why are they after you?" she asked.

Denying himself and denying her, he said again, "I don't know, people out of my past that I cannot remember anything about except a few names."

"Maybe you need to see one of our specialists at the hospital again," Peggy suggested.

"Let's talk about it later. Right now, I'd like to get some sleep." Orton wondered if Jack were still alive and if he was, was he looking for him. If true, Orton knew he'd have to deal with him when that time came.

"It would be nice to know something about your past

so we could tell our baby someday how his father grew up," Peggy said as she pushed Orton's pillow to one side and looked him in the eyes. "Did you hear me?"

"I heard you say baby! Did you say baby?"

"I said baby."

"Why didn't you tell me earlier?"

"I wasn't sure."

"At 2 a.m. you're sure?"

"Well, the tests results aren't in yet but I am pretty sure because my breasts are getting bigger don't you think?" Peggy lifted her night gown and exposed herself.

Orton smiled. "Yes, they are getting riper. I figured it was just a marriage thing or all that chocolate you've been eating."

Being a father was something Orton had come to terms with months earlier when he and Peggy had talked about it prior to their marriage. While he had his dead father's past to deal with, he knew that his love for Peggy was a bond that could overcome any obstacle. Perhaps dedicating his life to being the best possible father was a way to reconcile his past. Then, too, there was Doc Sutter. While he was his father-in-law, Orton saw him more as the real father he never had. He'd grown to respect and love this man. The fact that he could make Doc Sutter a grandfather gave Orton much pleasure, for he had seen the doctor with children in his care.

"Yes, that is a bit funny," Peggy said, "I never really

cared for chocolate and now I can't get enough of the stuff. But do you think I'm fat?"

"No, but I suspect between the chocolate and tiny Tim you're going to get there soon."

On August 17, 1943, some 230 American B-17 bombers tried to eradicate the ball bearing works in Schweifurt, Germany. Ball bearings made war machines run. Unfortunately, only 34 per cent of the factory was destroyed with a loss of 60 U.S. bombers from flak and German fighters. Each bomber had a seven-man crew. On one of those bombers was a turret gunner named Harry Whitman.

A week later a United States Army Air Force telegram letter showed up for a Mrs. Harry Whitman, Hayward, Wisconsin.Orton grabbed his route's mail and began sorting the letters into their assigned pigeonholes. When he came to the Whitman letter he stopped and held it in his hand. His hand began to shake. Bill Higgins, slotting mail for his route next to Orton's, looked over.

"Hey Jim, you okay, you don't look too good."

Jim looked up and slowly walked over and handed Higgins the letter. Higgins looked down at it.

"Oh no, oh God, no. Not Harry, oh God no, not Harry." Higgins sat down in his chair and began to weep. He and Whitman had been mail carriers together for six years starting right out of high school. Their wives were also close friends.

"You and I cannot deliver this letter," Orton said, "I'm going to get Cohen."

Postmaster Cohen came into the sorting room. "What's up boys? Hey, Bill, what the hell is going on?"

Higgins slowly handed the letter to Cohen. As soon as he saw the name and address, he took a deep breath. "Not a word of this to anybody until we deliver this letter," he commanded. Both men nodded. "Jim, take your car to the hospital and get Peggy, then pick up Bill's wife, Mary. I want the three of you to deliver the letter to Carol. Then leave the girls there and come back. I'll call the hospital and tell them that somethings come up, and Peggy is needed down here. Guys we still have to get this mail out."

Higgins quickly looked up at the two men. "Screw the damn mail. Harry's dead. Screw the damn mail. I may not deliver another god damn letter ever again. Harry's dead." In his chair he looked down at the floor and shook his head back and forth. "My mail buddy is gone," he said quietly, "and young Mr. Orton here now has a permanent job. Are you happy, Jim?"

"That was uncalled for Bill, and you know it," Cohen said angrily. "One more crack like that and your sub will have a permanent job. Now pull yourself together or go home. I can get your sub to fill in for you for a few days."

Bill Higgins got slowly out of his chair and walked out

of the post office. His substitute came in later, finished sorting the letters and delivered the mail.

Within hours after dropping Peggy and Mary Higgins at the Whitmans, the city of Hayward began mourning the loss of another one of their service men. Bill Higgins was found later that night in a drunken stupor on the bleachers of the local high school football field where he and Harry had once played. Harry was the quarterback, and Bill was his favorite receiver. Higgins returned to work three days later, stopping at Orton's desk, and apologizing for what he had said. Orton understood and shook his hand. From a slightly open office door, Cohen had watched the whole thing and let the matter rest.

With help from the local photography studio, Orton obtained a framed 8x10 picture of Airman Harry Whitman. He hung the photo on top of his mail slots much to the applause of the other mailmen. Bill Higgins had a sign made that said "Whitman's Way" and put it in the aisle between his desk and Orton's. The picture and sign remain there today.

The telegram letters that were sent to widows and families ended with Harry Whitman. He was the last serviceman to die from the Hayward area.

On his daily route, Orton often sat in his car and listened to mothers or wives as they read letters from their men overseas. As they read, he often wondered what if would have been like to take part in the epic battles that were going on. Because of his foot, no military service branch would take him. At the same time, he felt an obligation to be a direct part in keeping this country that he loved, his family and friends, too, free from the enemies that threatened them.

So, Jim Orton did what he could at home. He gave blood as often as he could. He organized metal scrap drives. On their small plot of land by the Namekagon River, they planted a garden and grew their own vegetables. He and Peggy purchased as many war bonds as they could afford. They put a sign in front of their house encouraging others to buy bonds. Much of that work came to a screeching halt one cold morning in January 1944.

"Jim, wake up," Peggy shook Orton hard. He was in one of his deep sleeps. "Wake up."

Drowsily he opened his eyes. "What time is it?"

"Two a.m. My water broke I'm going into labor. We're going to have a baby."

Orton had been preparing himself for this and, with his eyes still half closed, said, "Okay, wake me up when it's all over. Have fun."

Through the first wave of the pain, she grabbed a pillow and hit him hard with it. "Get up you idiot," and laughed through clenched teeth. "You're more than fifty per cent of this equation, Mr. Orton, so hop to."

He gently wrapped his arms around her and gave her a hug. "What can I do?"

"Call Daddy," she said, "he's been expecting this call. Then call the hospital and tell them we are on our way. Sue Beckman is the night nurse and knows my condition. Then get the car running; I don't trust that old truck. I checked the temp out there and its ten below zero. Throw a couple of quilts in it, too. You had better call your sub and tell her she's running the route today."

"That's quite a list," he said. "Anything else?"

"Yes, do it quick. This kid is starting to move."

Doc Sutter met Jim and Peggy at the emergency entrance. He immediately assessed that Peggy was ready to deliver his grandchild within the next few minutes. On the gurney going down the hallway, Peggy gave a loud scream, and a healthy push and Ronald James Orton came into the world. Doctor Ronald Sutter took his grandson and namesake from the bed. He cleared the mucous from its nose and gave the baby a slight whack on the rear. Young Ronald announced his entry.

Doc Sutter wanted to tell Jim that he was now the father of a healthy boy, but Orton had fainted when the baby screamed. Two orderlies helped Orton onto another gurney. The procession proceeded down the hall into a room. Mother, father, and child were soon under the care of the entire hospital staff all of whom would never let Orton forget his part in the delivery.

# 15

# THE KNIFE

"DAD, DAD," RONNIE LOOKED AT HIS FATHER WITH A TOUCH of disbelief. Jim Orton did not hear his son; he was staring down at a knife in his hand. On the blade was a long streak of blood from the deer he was standing over. It was the way this knife lay in his hand, the way it dripped the red fluid of life from the hilt down to the tip of the blade.

Orton had not thought about the kind of knife he had borrowed earlier from his friend John Thomas. Ronnie had forgotten his knife at home, so Jim gave his to his son and picked up John's for the hunt. When given, the knife had been in a dark stained leather sheath.

After he shot the young buck, he cut its throat to let it bleed. It was then that he found the knife in his hand, the same kind of knife he had used on his father years earlier.

You're gone, he thought, I buried you years ago in the sands of the Missouri river. You're gone.

In Orton's new world the knife dripped not the blood of the deer but the blood of his father. He was no longer in a wooded Wisconsin forest but along the river in Montana. Rather than a deer, he now gazed down on the lifeless body of his father. In the alkali dryness of the canyon the blood quickly hardened on the knife.

With bitter hate Orton looked down on the body. It was the father, Carl Wayland, who had devised the plan to kidnap the girl for ransom. When the girl was returned unharmed, they, along with brother Jack, would then run to Mexico and buy a ranch. Except for the elder Wayland, the plan would have succeeded. Maybe.

While waiting for a response from the girl's father, a Great Falls banker, Wayland's whiskey went to work. One afternoon he sent the boys out on a scouting mission. When they were gone, Carl had his way with the 15-year-old hostage. Although the girl was bound and gagged beneath a blanket, the boys took one look at their dad when they returned and knew what happened. Orton had reacted with quiet revulsion. Jack had only giggled.

The next day Wayland sent Jack to see about the money. Orton had feigned an injury and stayed behind for he knew what would happen if he left, knowing his father could not let the girl live after what he had done to her. The two fought. It ended when Orton put the knife into his father chest.

Like he had heard a hundred times in lurid dreams, Orton's father taunted him again, "I'm coming back for you son; Jack will find you." Orton, looking down on the knife in his hand, found new courage and said out loud, "I'll be waiting."

Ronnie touched his dad on the shoulder. "Waiting for what dad, waiting for what?"

Orton knew that his new courage was locked with the life and love he found with Peggy and his son. They were his existence which no evil could harm.

Orton smiled and looked at Ronnie. "I'm okay, Ronnie; I was thinking hard about an old deer I killed years ago."

"Would you tell me the story about that sometime?" Ronnie asked. He knew so little about his dad's past.

"Someday I will," Orton said, knowing he lied again. "Will you gut this deer out for me?"

"Sure dad," he said with a puzzled grin.

This was the first time Ronnie had field dressed a deer for his father. It had always been Orton's rule that whoever killed an animal field dressed it. Something is not quite right with dad, Ronnie thought. Like so many questions he had, Ronnie knew that maybe someday his dad might provide some answers. His mother had told him that Orton had suffered a brain injury and amnesia had blocked out much of his past memory.

Orton watched his son with pride. Ronny had learned this noble task well. He went about field dressing a deer with methodical thoroughness. The boy was more particular about cleaning the inside of an animal than Orton had been. Maybe, Orton thought, I put too much emphasis on that when I taught it to him. Maybe he has the instincts of a surgeon like his grandfather. Then again, a well-dressed deer made the family chore of cutting up the animal much more pleasant.

When Ronnie finished, they grabbed the stick with the rope that was fastened around the deer's neck and headed for the truck. Up and over small hills and grassy hummocks they pulled, occasionally stopping to catch their breaths or switch pulling sides.

At the truck both men got into the bed while holding onto the stick and pulled the animal up and onto the canvas liner.

"Did you see anything down by the cedar swamp?" Orton asked Ronnie as they climbed into the cab.

Ronnie cased his unloaded 30.06 rifle and put it behind his seat.

"Only two small ones," he replied, "so I waited for some adult supervision, but nothing showed up."

Adult supervision? Orton laughed. Where does he come up with this stuff? Must be his mother's wit. Orton looked at Ronnie and smiled. "You're the only one who needs adult supervision."

"Yup," Ronnie said, "and Becky Thomas just turned 16 and by law she's an adult in this state and she can supervise me all night long."

Now there is a statement he'd never make to his mother, Orton thought, concentrating on the gravel road. He knew Ronnie took some pride in dating this junior varsity cheerleader.

"All night? I don't think so." Orton said. "Now I know she has a car so I may have to talk to this young Thomas girl and tell her my son has to be home by nine o'clock."

Ronnie's eyebrows went up with his rising voice. "You and mom said 10 on weekends as long as my grades were good. Dad, you wouldn't say anything to Becka, would you?"

Orton laughed most of the way to the Sinclair station where they registered the deer and picked up some more gas.

"No, don't worry. I won't say anything to your Miss Becka," Orton said, putting Ronnie somewhat at ease again even though doubts lingered. Ronnie was fond of this girl and a fatherly intervention of any kind could mess things up permanent. When they hopped back into the truck Ronnie asked again to make sure.

"You wouldn't say anything would you?"

"No," Orton said with more laughter and Ronnie laughed, too.

On their way home, darkness began to close the day with only the headlights showing the road. Orton thought hard trying to remember if and when he and his father ever shared a laugh. Carl Wayland had only laughed when Orton was tripped by an unseen foot or when he'd made a mistake. His father laughed at young Orton's dreams of becoming a race car driver.

He dashed all thoughts of the dead man away and instead looked at Ronnie. Orton found himself living two lives. One was being a father to Ronnie and the other was reliving the carefree youth through his son that was denied him by his own father. A male wolf shows more affection for its pup than Wayland had shown towards him. Orton never knew why he bore the brunt of his father's wrath.

Peggy Orton waited for her boys to return. She figured one of them got a deer as they usually got home right after dark. Jim and Ronnie hunted on a friend's property a few miles south of Hayward. She had chicken stew simmering on the stove since 5 o'clock. It would have been venison, but they used up the last of last year's deer a month ago. The chicken came from one of their rogue roosters that Peggy never liked anyway.

November had been warmer than usual in Wisconsin this year making for a more pleasant deer hunt. There wasn't any tracking snow. Instead, there was a cold rain opening day and, with Ronnie suffering from a low-grade fever, they decided to go out Sunday when the rain was supposed to end. That morning Peggy packed sandwiches and sent her hunters on their way. She admired the care Jim took in teaching Ronnie how to hunt. It started at the age of ten when Jim dressed Ronnie in warm clothes and took him out to his stand on a wooded oak ridge. In breathless anticipation, Ronnie had not slept the night before. Peggy remembered that morning when young Ronnie got in the truck next to his dad and said,

"Dad, I've been waiting to do this my whole life."

For years Ronnie had pleaded with his dad to take him with him on the hunt. The lad had also taken an inherent interest in Jim's rifle shooting. The father had kept his son at bay until he couldn't stand it any longer. I'll take you when you turn ten was all he told the boy and you can hunt with a gun when you turn twelve. Peggy had watched this father-son thing with much amusement.

She often wondered how different it would have been had she and Jim had more children, perhaps two or three boys or a few girls. It was not to be. Six months after Ronnie was born, Peggy awoke one morning with a severe pain in her left side; she felt nauseous and weak. Jim called his mail route substitute to work for him and rushed Peggy to the hospital.

They were met at the emergency entrance by a Doctor

Paulson. Her father, Doctor Sutter was in Madison at a conference. On examination, Paulson found Peggy was suffering from an ectopic pregnancy where the egg does not attach itself to the walls of the uterus but instead grows elsewhere on the body. In Peggy's case it was on her cervix – a condition rare but dangerous to the mother.

Following surgery to remove the egg, Paulson sent Peggy to a specialist in Eau Claire. After a series of tests, it was found that her fallopian tubes were damaged, and she would be unable to have any more children.

The Ortons were crushed by the news. They had been looking forward to raising a big family. The specialist also told them it was lucky that Ronnie had been born at all. The night the two of them returned from Eau Claire Jim had another one of his recurring nightmares.

Again, the names of Wayland and Jack came up. And for the first time in his horrible dreams, Jim yelled out the name of a woman – "Sue Ann". When questioned the next morning, Jim said he could not remember any of those people or why they were haunting him.

Peggy Orton kept a diary. She had done it since her teen age years and kept up this daily journal much like her father kept notes on his patients. In Peggy's diary was now a collection of Jim's dreams. She knew they were the keys to a past he said he could not recall. But Peggy, now having been with this man for almost twenty years, knew different. Peggy suspected Jim was deliberately hiding a secret. What this kind gentle man had gone through she could not imagine. Years of prying yielded no answers. Jim Orton's past was a locked vault.

That past did not matter to Peggy. She loved and devoted herself to a man that she had cared for when he was taken off a train unconscious in 1938. He loved and cared for her in kind.

The Orton's new-but used pick up pulled into the driveway. Peggy was there to meet them. In the garage light she could see the legs of the deer sticking up out of the back of the truck. The two men got out and met her.

"So, which one of you two nimrods shot this big buck here?" she asked.

"It was dad's turn," Ronnie announced. "Remember I got one last year. I could have shot one too, but I didn't."

Orton jumped in. "You mean you could have shot two that together might have been as big as this one."

Ronnie grinned, "Maybe," he said. He took of his red cap and a shock of black hair fell over his dark eyes.

"You need a haircut young man," Peggy said in a commanding voice. "Tomorrow after school go down to Skelly's."

"Mom," he whined, "all the guys are starting to wear their hair longer."

"I'm not talking to all the guys. I'm talking to Ronald J Orton. Tomorrow!" she said.

"Okay," he said and started to walk toward the house.

"Wait a minute, Elvis, I'm going to need you and your mom's help here getting this deer on that overhead post in the garage. Do you recall where we left that winch?"

"Yeah, in the shed behind the garage," Ronnie said.

Orton left to get the winch.

"Mom," Ronnie said in a half whisper, "dad acted really strange today after he shot that deer. I found him standing over the deer with a bloody knife in his hand saying something like 'I'll be waiting.' He even made me gut his deer that he shot. He's never done that, and it's like he couldn't or wouldn't do it. It was weird."

Peggy looked at her son. "I don't know, Ronnie. Sometimes he can be a strange man. Don't worry about him, okay? He'll be fine."

"Sure Mom, I know," he said.

That night Peggy added what Ronnie had told her to the diary.

# 16

# JACK

THE DEER SEASON ENDED WITHOUT SNOW BUT THE COLD returned. The Ortons butchered their deer, wrapped the meat in waxed paper, and placed most of it in their small freezer. Doc Sutter's freezer would hold what they couldn't store, and Jim enjoyed the thought of supplying his father-in-law with venison.

After dropping off the meat and having a beer with Doc, Jim made his way down Highway 63 and was about to turn south on 27 when he noticed an older model green chevy truck with Montana licenses plates in the parking lot across from the Moccasin Bar. A rifle rack with a 30-30 Winchester hung from the window. As he drove past the truck in the lot Orton could see dangling from the rear-view mirror two pink rabbit's feet on a chain. He knew of only one man who cherished those odd good luck charms - Jack Wayland.

So, this was it. After almost 20 years his brother had caught up to him to even the score. Gripping the steering wheel tight, Orton drove behind the newspaper office and parked his truck. He walked over into the shadows of the front doorway and watched and waited. The cold dry wind didn't bother him. His adrenaline coursed hot blood through him. He began to sweat. After all these years the nightmare took the shape and form of a beat-up looking cowboy who had exited the Moccasin now and walked toward his truck. It was Jack. Same kind of hat, same kind of silver tipped cowboy boots, same kind of half a leg shuffle in his walk.

The lone figure in the ragged dirty Stetson looked up and down the street as if unsure of his next move. Orton watched. A rising fear took hold, his heart raced almost outpacing his thoughts. Should I kill him here, now? Should I follow him to where he might be staying the night and confront him there? What if Jack drives to my home? If that should happen, I would have to deal with him before Jack would get into the house. The home where the two most important people in my life live. He couldn't allow that. But in his heart of hearts, Orton knew he could not kill again unless Peggy and Ronnie were threatened. A city patrol car drove by. Keep going Orton thought. The car continued up main.

Jack made his way to his truck, got in and headed south. Orton quickly ran back to his truck and followed. It was easy. One taillight on the green Chev was out. A mile outside of town he saw Jack turn into a motel and watched as he made his way to the office.

Good, Orton thought. Jack will spend the night here and come looking for me in the morning. He stayed long enough to ensure that Jack took his case into his room and settled in. Orton drove home.

Unseen by Orton or Jack was a shiny black car with Montana plates watching from across the road in a pull off near the railroad tracks. Inside were two men and a woman.

Orton would call his mail route substitute and request that she deliver for him tomorrow. He'd tell Peggy he wasn't feeling well. He'd then stay home and wait for Jack to show up. He would show up and Orton had no idea of how he would deal with him.

Tuesday morning dawned cold and clear. A black Buick dropped a middle-aged woman and a young man off at the entrance to the hospital and sped away. The woman and man walked up to the hospital desk and asked for the pharmacy. Peggy Orton was on duty at the desk filling in for another nurse.

"What do you need ma'am?" she asked.

"My son has asthma and somehow, he left his medicine at home, and he seems to be in some distress. I have the name of his medicine here," the woman said, showing Peggy the drug's name that was written down on a piece of paper.

Peggy studied it a moment and said, "I cannot release this drug without approval from a doctor."

"Oh, for God's sake," she said, "I can get this drug at any corner Rexall in Great Falls, Montana, and you're telling me I need a doctor's okay here? My son needs this medicine now."

It was a common drug, but for some reason this hospital had a no-release policy without a doctor's approval for it. "I am sorry ma'am; that is our policy. Let me page Doctor Paulson, he is our on-staff physician. I am sure he can help you right away. Now can I have your name?" Peggy asked.

"Yancy, Sue Ann Yancy," she said.

"Okay Miss Yancy I'll, I'll," Peggy hesitated. She looked at the woman. She couldn't speak.

"Are you alright nurse?" Miss Yancy asked. "You look like you have seen a ghost."

"Did you say you were from Montana?" Peggy asked.

"Yes, I did, Great Falls to be exact." It was then that Yancy noticed the name tag on Peggy's uniform. "Odd, we are here looking for a man named Orton, Orton Wayland," she said.

"You mean like Jack Wayland or Carl Wayland?" Peggy asked.

Sue Ann Yancy was stunned. She looked at her son and back to Peggy. "How did you know those were the people I, my son here and my detective are looking for? Who are you?"

At that moment the young man with asthma began to inhale but could not catch his breath. He coughed but could hardly exhale. Peggy ran back to the pharmacy and came back with the drug Miss Yancy needed and gave them to her. She grabbed a cup of water from behind the counter and offered it to the young man as he downed two of the pills. Within a minute, the wheezing subsided and he could take a full breath.

"Thank you," he said, "thank you."

The desk nurse returned.

"Christine," Peggy said, "I am taking these two people into conference room 3 for a consultation. If anyone asks for Sue Ann Yancy or me that is where we will be."

Orton checked the back of the house. He figured Jack would not be so brazen as to attempt a front door entry. On the kitchen table was his 308 deer rifle; next to it was a magnum 22 single-action pistol. Both were loaded. The kitchen area was flooded with morning light, but the living room and back bedrooms were dark with the shades drawn. The house was eerily quiet.

I've got some money set aside, Orton thought as he sat at the table watching the front and back doors. Maybe I can bribe Jack with it to leave me and my family alone.

Peggy didn't know about that money. Orton had gotten it over the years from patron's tips on his mail route, usually at Christmas time. If and when his brother did return, he might have some bargaining money. Should Jack never return for some reason, Orton could surprise Peggy with a vacation in Florida, something she had mentioned to him a few times, a getaway for a week or two, she said, to shorten the long Wisconsin winters. The amount he'd put away was substantial enough to buy a new truck if Jack never showed up. However, his brother was back, and Orton had to deal with him.

It bothered Orton, this money secret he withheld from Peggy. It was bad enough that he'd kept the lie about his past from her, but this was new between them. She trusted him. He was afraid that if she ever found out about the hidden cash, she might be angry enough to leave him. No, she wouldn't do that, but she would be hurt and part of that loving bond would be broken. He was humbled in a way; she loved him and he had returned it tenfold. This lie about the money tore into the depths of his soul, and he cursed his father and brother for causing it. Orton gritted his teeth. Damn you, Jack. Why couldn't you have just left me alone?

A knock at the front door interrupted his thoughts. Orton picked up the pistol and held it down by his side. He walked quietly to the door and looked out a side window. He could see a young man holding some newspapers. The kid knocked again. Orton set the pistol down on the couch and answered the door.

"Mister, you want to buy a Grit newspaper?" the youth asked.

"No, I don't," Orton replied.

"Oh, okay, a man down the street said you'd buy one from me. Okay then goodbye," the little paper boy said and walked back down the steps.

Orton shook his head and watched the lad go, as he turned back into the room, he was met by Jack standing in the kitchen holding a big 45 caliber six gun. It looked familiar.

"You don't lock your doors very well, brother," Jack said with a smile, "and don't bother to go for that little pea shooter on the couch. This big boy here will blow you away before you get close to it."

The rifle lay on the table behind Jack.

"It's been 20 years Jack. What do you want? Why did you come for me?" Orton asked.

Jack backed up to the table, grabbed the rifle and sat down. "In here and join me. We have a lot to talk about. I want to get reacquainted with my long-lost brother."

Orton, always keeping his eyes on Jack, walked in and sat down. Jack leveled the old Colt at Orton's chest.

"You got any whiskey?"

"No."

"Any hooch of any kind?"

"No."

"First off," Jack said, "I want to know what you did with all that money you got from ransoming that girl because they never paid me. They said they were still getting all that money together. When I left, they followed and caught me holed up at the Missouri Breaks shack.

"You, dad, and the girl were gone. I had it in mind that the two of you double crossed me and went for the money yourselves. Luckily, I made my way out the back and escaped through a side canyon. Dad showed me that get away. Anyway, after I got to a safe place, I realized that dad would never take up with you and leave me hanging. He despised you, Orton, like I did.

"So, you must have got the drop on dad and killed him and ransomed the girl for yourself. I read later in the newspapers that the girl was returned unharmed, a bit shaken from her whole ordeal, but alive. There was no mention of the ransom so that all must have been hushed up and gone to you. God, I hated you then as I hate you now. So, what the hell did you do with all that money Orton?"

Jack's voice continued to rise as he spoke, and some of the tobacco he was chewing came spitting out his mouth. Flecks of it stained Peggy's white cotton tablecloth.

"I ain't leaving here without it. Your sorry ass took from me two things I wanted most in my life. One, a ranch in Mexico, and two, a chance for Dad and I to romp it up where the law wouldn't get us. Now, I plan to take two things from you that you value most if I don't get that $20,000. One, your life, and two, whoever walks through that door at the end of this day goes with you to the hell you deserve! I also want to know what you did with Dad, and I want the truth."

Orton was only half listening. He tried to think of how he could get Jack's gun or his rifle before he died from Jack's gun shot. He was going to risk his life to ensure no harm came to Peggy or Ronnie. They were two innocent people who were unfortunate to fall in with one of Carl Wayland's sons. When Peggy came home tonight, she would find him and some cowboy dead on the floor. She would never know why. This was the price he would pay for killing his father regardless of the fact it saved another life.

"I can get you $5,000 of the money right now, Jack. The rest I can send to you over time wherever you are," Orton said. "You can buy a place in Mexico like you want and then you can live on the money I send to you every couple of months. This deal I can promise you. What do you say?"

Jack gritted his teeth and snarled, "You didn't hear me, I want all that money right now. Not some, all." He fingered the cocking mechanism on his gun. "What happened to dad?"

For Orton it was time. "After you left to get the ransom Dad was going to get the girl and kill her. He had raped her several times, and he knew he couldn't let her live. So yes, we got into a fight, and I killed him and buried him in the sand along the river. I then took the girl to a ranch house down the road. I left her with the ranchers and fled. I didn't stop to collect any ransom money. That is the truth of it, Jack. But I do have some money, and I will pay you back what you think your fair share is. Just let me and my family be."

"You know, Orton, you are a good liar," Jack yelled. "I believe you killed pa but you didn't get all this here (he looked around the rooms) without some kinda' start up poke. So, I think you got the ransom money, and you came and found a nice quiet out of the way town in this cold ass state they call Wisconsin. You've got quite a place here, brother, and from the looks of the pictures on the wall a nice woman and kid. None of that means a damn to me. For 20 years I been scrimping along and looking for you. As luck would have it, I ran into two drunks in Malta who remembered beating up a young guy and tossing him into a train car headed this way. You must have had the money in your boots."

Jack laughed. "Must have made you look tall. You have all that money stashed in this house somewhere. So first I'm going to kill you and then I'll find the money and then I'll have a chat with..." Jack never finished the sentence.

He felt the cold steel of a gun at the back of his neck.

"Put the gun down slowly Mr. Wayland," the voice behind him said. Jack did as he was told. A big man in a dark suit then grabbed Jack's gun off the table and put it in his waist belt.

"I've got to agree with your brother, Jack, here," said the man to Orton. "You don't know how to lock your house up. I found it amazingly easy to get into your bedroom through the window. Being a former police detective, I could show you a thing or two about home security. I listened to this whole show. Answered a ton of questions my employer and I had. Mr. Orton, Wayland, would you be so kind sir as to take these keys to the big black Buick down the street and go to the hospital and pick up Miss Sue Ann Yancy and her son. Me and Mr. Jack here will wait until you get back. Tell her Dawson sent you. She'll understand."

# 17

# DAWSON

JIM ORTON SAT IN THE BIG BLACK BUICK WITH A THOUSAND thoughts cramming his head. A man he had never met was holding his brother. So this man, Dawson, could explain to a woman he, Jim Orton had helped kidnap twenty years ago, explain to her what? That Jack was responsible for the whole kidnapping? Would I go to jail for helping to aid and abet this crime? It was I who picked up Sue Ann Yancy in Great Falls. Could I be held for the murder of my father? Dawson had heard me confess that crime to Jack. What was Dawson, an ex-policeman, going to do with Jack while I was going to get Sue Ann Yancy? Shouldn't I take this car and drive to Canada or flee to some other part of the world where no one would ever find me? This detective knows I cannot hide from him. They have Jack. Would they be satisfied only with him? But wait, Dawson knew no ransom was paid. Dawson believed every word I said. He trusts me somehow....

Walking into the hospital he checked the waiting area. No one was around. As he turned toward the front desk he bumped into Christine.

"Jim, are you looking for Peggy?" she asked.

"Ah, no, I am looking for a Sue Ann Yancy."

"Oh, well, she's with Peggy in conference room three."

"Peggy's with Sue Ann Yancy? What?"

Orton ran over to the room. He feared Sue Ann Yancy might be seeking some kind of revenge for his former misdeed. He tore open the door. There he found Peggy holding the hand of Sue Ann Yancy. A young man, who looked familiar, was sitting next to Sue Ann.

Peggy looked up surprised and said, "Jim what are you doing here?"

"Are you okay? Has this woman hurt you in anyway?"

"No, don't be silly. What are you doing here?"

He couldn't think of anything to say other than "Dawson sent me to pick up Sue Ann."

Sue Ann looked up at Orton and smiled. "My Dawson sent you?"

"Yes, he said you would understand."

"What I know is, is that I trust Dawson implicitly, and if he has sent you then he must have your brother Jack with him, and, Mr. Orton or Wayland, he trusts you, and so do I."

The young man next to Sue Ann spoke. "Mother, isn't this one of the men who kidnapped you? Shouldn't Dawson have handcuffed him?"

Sue Ann looked at her son. "If Dawson sent him to get us, we go with him, no questions asked."

Peggy stared at Jim. Her face was one of anger, pity, and love.

"Peggy," Jim said to her, "there is so much I have to tell you. And I will."

Sue Ann broke in. "I've a feeling, Miss Orton, that if it wasn't for your man here I wouldn't be alive today. Isn't that right Mr. Orton?"

As tears began to fill Jim's eyes, they met Peggy's. "Yes," he said nodding his head, and then turning to Sue Ann he said, "Yes."

"C'mon, let's go," Sue Ann said, "mustn't keep Dawson waiting."

Peggy said, "I'm going too. I want to meet your brother, this man of your nightmares. I want to find out why he has haunted you all these years."

The four of them drove to the Ortons. They entered the side door into the kitchen. Jack sat with his hands on the table. Dawson stood behind him with a gun. Peggy was behind Jim as they came in. As they all entered Dawson looked up for a moment and Jack saw his chance. He swung a fist toward the gun that knocked it out of Dawson's hand. Jack then grabbed the .308 rifle that was sitting next to him and leveled it at Peggy. He pulled the trigger. Nothing happened. Jim quickly grabbed the rifle barrel and pulled it up out of the way with his left hand. His right fist crashed into Jack's jaw. Jack went down, spitting his last remaining teeth. Dawson was on top of him with a pair of handcuffs. He pulled Jack back up into the chair with his pistol into the cheek of a bloodied face. "One move and it is your last."

"Damn," Dawson said. "I should have cuffed him after you left Orton; I am sorry."

Jack mumbled, "I think he broke my jaw."

"If you can talk, your jaw is not broken," Peggy said.

"Orton, didn't dad teach you to always leave the safety off your guns?" Jack mumbled.

"Maybe in your house but not in this one," Jim said seething with rage and a hope that Jack would make another move so Dawson would finish Jack once and for all.

Jim went to hit Jack again, but Peggy grabbed his arm and stopped him. "Jim don't; he can't hurt us now. It's all over."

Sue Ann and her son Jim came into the kitchen that was soon getting crowded.

Dawson said, "Maybe you all should find a place in the living room. I can speak from here. Now I know everyone here except this young lady," nodding to Peggy.

"This is my wife, Peggy, Mr. Dawson, "Jim said.

"Glad to meet you ma'am." Looking into the living room he said, "Miss Yancy, this is what I have learned over the years from my investigation of your kidnapping, and, of late, listening to Jack and his brother talk which put all of the pieces of this ungodly crime together. It appears that...."

"Orton planned the whole thing. It was all his idea," Jack yelled out.

Dawson grabbed a large sheet of cotton cloth from his pocket and gagged Jack's mouth. With a piece of rope, he tied Jack's head to the back of the chair. Jack couldn't move.

"As I was saying," Dawson continued, "It was Carl Wayland, these boys' father, who planned to kidnap you for ransom Sue Ann. They were then going to take the ransom money and go to Mexico and buy a ranch. Jack here was all for the plan, but I believe brother Orton didn't want to be part of it. Jack confessed to me a few minutes ago before you all got here that neither he nor Carl trusted Orton and kept a gun on him most of the time. Anyway, Carl sent Jack to get the ransom money. But of course the police, of which I was a detective on the case at the time, told Jack it would take another week to get the money. Jack then went back to the hideout, and we followed. We had thought we had the whole gang cornered in the Missouri Breaks shack but, somehow, they all escaped. We still don't know how to this day they got away. Then Sue Ann, a few days later, you showed up at the Gunderson's ranch. They said some sandy haired, blue-eyed boy dropped you off and sped into the night. I believe that was Orton. Isn't that right Orton?"

Jim, with a distant look in his eyes as he remembered the events of that evening, glanced at Dawson and then Sue Ann and nodded his head yes. Peggy put his arm around Jim and hugged him.

"It appears that after he left the Gunderson's, Orton was going to catch a train and head east maybe to get lost in one of the big cities. Isn't that right, Orton?"

Again, Jim nodded yes.

"But two guys at the Malta Montana train station jumped Orton, took what little money he had from working for a lumberman, and threw him in a boat that ended up here in Hayward."

"And that's where we found you," Peggy said.

Jim squeezed Peggy's hand. "I guess I got lucky there." He looked at her and smiled.

Dawson addressed the Ortons. "Miss Yancy hired me to find out who violated and almost killed her. She said she would not rest until those three men were found and tried. I've since also become her Chief of Security at her banks. Anyway, underneath one of the beds in the Breaks cabin I found one name, Wayland. So, I and the Yancys have been following Jack after we picked up his trail in Colorado after a bank heist. We were hoping that he would lead us to you or Carl. When we hit Hayward behind Jack, I did some checking on you Orton. You seem to be a square dude and, in my estimation, a real gentleman who unfortunately got throwed into a bad lot."

"So then, what happened to Carl Wayland?" Sue Ann Yancy asked.

"Well, it appears that Orton..." Dawson started to explain, but Orton cut in.

"Hold on Dawson, let me tell this. I want Peggy to know from me what happened. I think I owe that to her. I've been feigning amnesia all these years out of fear that should anyone find out what I did I might go to jail for it. I don't care now."

Looking hard into Peggy's eyes, Jim said, "Please forgive me for not telling you all this. I was so afraid... I have been so afraid. You see after Dad, Carl, sent Jack to get the ransom money that morning, he had his way with Sue Ann one more time. It occurred to me that because of what he did he would not let her live. I confronted him about it. He said he was going to kill her and so we fought. He had been drinking so that slowed his reactions a bit and I got the best of him. Somehow the knife I had been carrying found its way into my hand. I used it to kill him. He is buried deep in the sands along the river."

Orton began to shake, adding "But he keeps coming back to me."

Peggy remembered parts of his dreams and the recent incident with the knife and the deer this past season. It started to become clearer what Jim had been going through. She again put her arms around her man. "It's okay, Jim, I understand. You did what you had to do. I love you, Jim. Nothing will change that. I am so much a part of you now that, whatever happens, I'll be there with you. Your father won't be coming back because the two of us will bury him in our past forever."

"Yes, yes, we will." Jim smiled "Oh god how I love you woman."

Dawson spoke, "Miss Yancy, how do you want to proceed?"

Pointing at Jack she said, "Well I want you to get this piece of dung out of the Orton's home. We will take him back and him alone to Montana to stand trial for my kidnapping. As far as I'm concerned, he is the only one who did it. Then we will hand him over to the law in Colorado where he's wanted for killing a bank teller in a hold up. They still hang people for murder in that state, and I have friends there in high places that can ensure that gets done. I don't ever want that man to come back and bother these good people again."

Before he untied Jack from the chair, Dawson chain shackled his ankles. He then led Jack out to the car.

Sue Ann continued: "To me, Carl Wayland and Orton Wayland never existed. From what we can gather there are no records of any of you. But I will remember a man named Jim Orton who saved my life and for that I will be eternally grateful. If Jim or Peggy Orton or any of the Orton's need anything, all they have to do is get a hold of me or my son here.

"You see, Jim, I came out of that whole ordeal a stronger woman determined to retake my new life head on, and I did. My dad left me two banks, and I added three more along with part ownership in a railroad. By the way, there is a $5,000 reward in Colorado for Jack Wayland. Because we found him in your house, I plan to give you that reward, maybe help pay for your Ronnie's college or something. And, Peggy, maybe you should go back into all those diaries of yours and black out any reference to Jack or Carl. As I said, those men don't exist."

"What diaries?" Jim asked.

"What do you think all those boxes of little books are in the basement? "she explained. "I've been keeping a daily diary since I was a little girl. And I just happen to record all those names and incidents from the nightmares that you have had over the years. That's what Sue Ann and I were talking about when you came into the conference room. I was hoping that somewhere along I might be able to put all of them together to figure out what happened to you because you sure wouldn't tell me. I suspected you knew all along."

"But you didn't confront me with it?"

"No, I love you too much. I believed that when the time was right, you would tell me."

"And I would have."

"I know."

"There's so much more I have to tell you."

"We will have time for that."

Sue Ann gave Jim Orton a hug. With tears in her eyes she said, "Thanks again for the courageous thing you did. I am sorry for all the hell it has caused you over these years." She then gave Peggy a hug. "My dear, you've got one helluva guy here. Take good care of him."

"I know that, and I will," Peggy said.

Sue Ann turned to her son, "Let's go, Jim my boy. We have a long drive a head of us."

Orton went to shake Jim Yancy's hand. "You sure look familiar. Have we met?"

"No, I've never been in Wisconsin, ever," he said. "C'mon mom let's go."

"Wait, there is one more thing you should know, Mr. Orton," Sue Ann said.

"Mom don't."

"They need to know son. Mr. Orton here would eventually suspect it."

"Please Mom, don't."

"You see my son here is your half-brother."

"Ooooh, Mom."

"So, I guess that makes up all somewhat related," Sue Ann said happily. "Trust me. We'll be in touch."

Jim Yancy shrugged his shoulders and shook his

head. "Okay, I guess. It is time to go, Mom."

The two Yancys went out the door, leaving Jim and Peggy alone.

"Well, I'll be damned," Jim said, shaking his head.

"Jim don't swear in this house."

"Sorry. Hey, I need some air. This whole thing has made me feeling a bit light headed."

Jim went out the back door and onto the deck. Peggy followed. Down and away, the Namekagon River sparkled in the sun. A thousand diamonds of light kissed the waters below. Like long fur on a running shaggy dog, the big mature white and red pines swayed in a gentle breeze. The early December wind was cold, but Jim Orton didn't notice. He turned and took a shivering Peggy into his arms.

"How would you like to go to Florida for a few weeks this winter?" he asked.

"Jim! I'd love to; however, you know we can't afford that, and we are not using that ransom money. That belongs to Ronnie."

He looked into her big brown eyes and smiled, "I agree with you. But..."

"But what?"

"Well, there's one more big, really big thing I've got to tell you."